MW00790973

A

SWEET
DEATH

by Claude Tardat

translated from the French by Erin K. Wilson

Chromatophore Press
Seattle, Washington

Copyright © 2010, 2017 by Claude Tardat
Translation Copyright © 2010, 2017 Erin K. Wilson

All English rights reserved. Published in the United States by Chromatophore Press.

No part of this book may be reproduced in any manner whatsoever without prior written permission, except in the case of brief quotations embodied in critical articles or reviews.

Cover Design & Book Interiors: Vladimir Verano

CHROMATOPHORE PRESS

4131 Brooklyn Avenue NE #108
Seattle, Washington 98105

ISBN: 978-1-60944-015-2

PRODUCED BY THIRD PLACE PRESS
LAKE FOREST PARK, WASHINGTON
www.thirdplacepress.com

3

A Sweet Death

S unday. A nasty day.

Sunday is always a big empty hole in the middle of my stomach, a void that all the sweetshops in the world couldn't begin to fill. At tea time, between the digestive torpor of noon and the boredom of the encroaching evening, I'll get a distinct craving for frangipane[1], golden with its egg-white glaze. It is a day for doing nothing. It is dedicated to the warmth of sleeping in, and dreams from which I cannot escape. To a parade of meticulously crafted desserts, a harvest reaped from hot ovens.

It is a day for doing nothing, just like any other. A day for sugar, a day filled with terrible longings. I want the sugar to fulfill its task. And then, my body will float away on a river of syrup. And at the mouth of the river, death will put an end to the clinging elasticity of Sundays. I will float along, a candied island, weightless upon the eternal sweetness of honey.

—

What to do? Maybe I'll go to the movies.

—

Night, between Sunday and Monday.

In the semi-darkness of the nearly empty cinema, the chocolate Kim Cone[2] slides down my neck and onto my skirt in thick, devastating rivulets. The stifling heat keeps me from catching the dribbling morass of ice cream that paints my clothes with a dark, fishy mottling. The precious substance sticks the fabric to my thighs: one more missed pleasure. If I were slim and supple, I could simply bend my head to my knees and lick up the flowing chocolate. But my tongue is permanently exiled from the rest of my body. I lift my skirt, wipe up the sticky mixture of sugar and sweat with a finger and taste it. The salt of my perspiration ruins the flavor of the chocolate. What a pity.

The hackneyed images of a film that doesn't interest me flash across the screen. Some no-name actress, platinum blonde and with generous curves (but nothing so generous as mine) is trying to seduce the supposedly incorruptible hero. It is excruciatingly vulgar, and so boring that people are walking out. They leave with no discretion whatsoever, one after the other, displaying their discontent. I don't care. I'm not here for the movie, but for the candy and Eskimo Pies at intermission. For the unsettling sensation of completely anonymous gorging in the depth of these theater seats. For the dance of lips along the edge of an ice cream bar or a cone. For the mad race of the tongue against ice cream that melts too quickly.

Thanks to a scene in the open desert under the white light of an implacable sun, I can survey the full extent of the damage to my skirt. I also enjoy the thought of the striking image I will probably present to the world in full daylight. The people in line for the next show will note the passage of a hideous little creature, stuffed like a sausage into her elasticized clothing. Garments the color of a dirty bib.

When the lights come up, I go out and expose myself to an avalanche of glances. They hit their mark: rapid, surreptitious, discreet as possible but frequently repeated. They don't dare inspect me from head to toe, for fear I might notice.

And they think: "Such negligence, such slovenliness! How does she live? In her state you'd think she'd at least tidy herself up a little…"

No one has the least idea that behind this front lies a conscious will, an organizing principle. Who could look at the chocolaty grimace I throw before the beatific aestheticism of those who love life, and find it beautiful?

———

Tuesday. Middle of the night.

Alone with my thunderous gulping. My nibbling is amplified by the nocturnal silence. A horrid cacophony of mastication. I know the entire range of possible noises, having eaten so often in solitude. I listen to the sugar's long pilgrimage through me. It has the slowness of a funerary march, filling the time I still have left to bloat.

When I was little, I would shut my eyes during meals on the rare occasions I was allowed to sit with the grown-ups. Their mouths broadcast terrifying sounds: rotary presses, band saws, waterfalls, trains moving at all speeds, buzzing insects. Slow, tranquil, lazy, frenetic rhythms. An obscene animal music made by rodents with human faces.

How noisy the body is when you think to listen to it. And what enigmatic company.

—

Thursday evening.

Rue de Rivoli, in a tea-room with a predominately female clientele. Powdered old ladies, accessorizing with shaved poodles or tiny Chihuahuas, sipping thick bitter chocolate served in the grand tradition of the 18th century. Unless you add sugar, the cocoa is completely undrinkable. Not that I'd ever put it in my cup! The afternoon has been delicious. Installed smack in the middle of the vast room, my buttocks overflowing the seat of the Voltaire armchair, I am the focal point for all these women: the queen of ugliness and of gluttony, already ageless and featureless. I am devoted solely to the pleasures of chocolate and petit-fours drenched in Grand Marnier. I am more scandalous and undesirable in this operatic décor than even those bored and slobbering doggies that quiver with lust upon bejeweled bosoms. If the management hasn't issued me a direct order to vacate the premises it is by the grace of my Dior blouse and a few thoughtfully distributed tips. Must I place myself under the protection of the great couture houses to gain entrance to the garden of delights? Must I exhibit myself to luxury clothiers—even though I despoil their prestigious work—in order to be accepted on the same footing as these ludicrous representatives of the canine race, festooned with braided leather and velvet ribbons? Must I be forced to invest money in sartorial celebrity, money which could instead have been dedicated exclusively to sugar? Such is the way of the world, which embraces imperfection and deformity as long as they come with a designer label.

—

Mama has always chosen my wardrobe, with no real regard for my comfort or tastes. Petrified during preparations for children's Masses, I was then joined by other kids just as stiff and strained as me at these rare ceremonies. A few photos attest to my nascent monstrosity, as well as my utter inability to display even the remotest degree of elegance while decked out in my Sunday best.

With subtle cuts and carefully selected colors, some the couturiers in Mama's circle have lately tried to mitigate my plumpness, a task requiring both imagination and ingenuity. No luck. The unworthy daughter of a woman who can inspire artists to devise the most audacious creations, I immediately give each new frock the appearance of a sack stuffed with hay, too narrow to resist the pressure of its contents.

—

Saturday.

Time to launder my carcass at the neighborhood bath-house. It is a matter of necessity. At home, it's the faucet at the end of the hall, a furtive wash on the landing, very late at night when the neighbors all seem to be asleep. Or I lug an over-full basin back to my room, trying not to spill. This is getting more and more difficult — clumsiness has accompanied my increasing weight.

The bath-houses reek of chlorinated vapors that eat the taste of sugar away from my mouth. The lights glare. My body, wedged into a microscopic shower stall, is the color of the undead. Glazed white tiles as far as the eye can see. Like a morgue. I have never set foot in a morgue, but this is exactly how I think it would look.

Maybe the dormitory showers are less sinister. I can use them if I want. But no — I am revolted by the promiscuity of the students. It's enough we have to see each other in the lecture halls.

And I would no doubt crack all the mirrors.

—

Sunday.

This unintended journal, which I began without really even noticing, is the result of the invasive silence of the night, and of the tenacious weight sitting in the pit of my gut.

A Sweet Death

Soon I will be twenty years old. That age or another—
what's the big deal? The days are all alike, the seasons are
all making me flabby and limp, and I have no story to tell.
Nothing but asinine facts, recorded each day to simulate
having a life. Time is already carved in stone. I have
always been old. Or at least ageless.

Since I have it, this journal may as well be the record of
my death, as it simmers over a low flame. I have elected
to meet my demise by certain but agreeable means. They
are a bit disgusting, yes, but they are my own. My way of
distinguishing myself. I have made a solemn vow to myself
to commit premeditated suicide: with sugar.

Is it really necessary to set a date? Because every day is
another day of sugar.

———

At the university, in the morning.

"Great literary sensibility. Acute analysis. Elegant style."

The professor in my Comparative Literature class
blanketed my latest paper with compliments like these.
I'd prefer he say something along the lines of, "A massive
lump of lard, but shows some talent." That would amuse
me. But no one would ever dare. It's certainly what they
think—all these students, simultaneously skeptical and
envious. Their vaguely distressed gazes converge upon me
as the teacher cites passages from my homework. If they
only knew how easy it is for me to unravel their secret
thoughts. And if they only knew just how little I care
about this paper, that grade, these compliments! Behind

a smokescreen of geniality, I think of other things: the bar of raisin-studded chocolate I'm going to buy when I leave here, to celebrate yet another absurdly meaningless academic success.

At the door, one of them asks if he can borrow my notes from a class that he missed. Me—the unapproachable and the unapproached, cocooned within my eiderdown of cellulite and silence. And yet here is someone who has sought me out, who has come up and spoken to me, asked me questions. A professor loaded with degrees and references publicly reveals my little parcel of genius and suddenly everyone is trying to stroke the monster the right way, to cover her in flattery and attention. Well, it is always useful to curry favor with the best. You never know, do you? But this spontaneity and impartiality is only an illusion.

The Student invited me for a drink in the cafeteria. A way of thanking me for the use of my notes, of course. But I said no. I was in too much of a hurry to get back to my sugar. Besides, I have nothing to say to him, or to anyone. I don't know how to talk to people. I learned the treachery of speech very early on in life. The sincerity of the written word? I'll trust that in a pinch. Sometimes.

I got a nougat bar from a vending machine on the subway platform. I nibbled at it as I went back up the Rue de Rome. This evening's meal shall consist of the delights of a Saint-Honoré[3] and an amandine[4].

—

The family apartment. It's always deserted when I come to visit. My father is never there. He's off diplomatizing somewhere. Probably to avoid seeing me. At least I had the decency to give them advance warning. Mama always arranges not to have any callers this particular day so Zohra can have the day off. And so nobody risks running into me. Prodigious progeny, defiling the living room. I suppose I make them ashamed. Mama keeps quiet, ever the stoic, never broaching the subject. We sit and have a bite to eat, we chat about literature. She has been helping me study. In the afternoon I am subjected to a tedious fitting session. A seamstress has come to take my measurements for some new style intended to lengthen my silhouette and conceal my shape. Not a single word—ever—about my superfluous weight. From one fitting to the next, they always have to let seams out, enlarge the skirts and dresses. Pants have been summarily eliminated from my stock of clothing. It's not my idea to have a nice wardrobe. None of these styles—supposedly so advantageous to my figure—are my idea either. But I play the game. Forcing the challenges of my misshapenness upon my mother satisfies my exhibitionist tendencies, and helps me forget the fatigue of standing up for the entire fitting session.

When I was with Mama today she was silent yet again on the essential point: my ever-increasing weight. But there have been some unmistakable looks. A hint of embarrassment. A vague repulsion. The tiniest suggestion of her sense of powerlessness in simply getting to the root of the problem.

After I leave, I hurry into a pastry shop with a hunger gnawing at my soul, and devour an enormous raisin pudding.

—

Rain over Paris. Glistening sidewalks. Water trickling endlessly down the window of the café where I have ensconced myself to write. A long while back I emptied a large cup of frothy cocoa. The last drop left a beauty mark on the edge of the saucer. If I moisten my fingertip I can collect all the crumbs that are strewn across the tablecloth. The customers who have come in to shelter from the rain throw me that awkward glance generally reserved for the handicapped and the infirm. They don't want to have this look, but too late—they've had it, and they can see that I've seen them. They can't act as if I'm not there. I have been indelibly seen. The rudiments of my femininity, swaddled in fat, have been seen. The obese little monster, who continues feeding her eighty-kilo frame, has been seen. The stubborn girl, who quit growing at a meter and a half in height, but keeps expanding in girth so as to go unnoticed, has been seen. For a few seconds, I have a place in their minds. That is the incomparable privilege of my situation. I inflict embarrassment upon them. And that pleases me.

—

Mama does not age. She is always a very beautiful woman.

—

A meter and a half. Not a centimeter taller. I checked again this morning. The figure is there. A round figure. That pleases me.

—

My mother is a genius when it comes to literature. She has acquitted herself brilliantly in her role as my private tutor. Thanks to her, I have been spared the constricted scholastic view of books and art. But she has never spent even one minute with me beyond the time she had scheduled for my lessons. She was very patient with me during those two hours a day during which she initiated me into the mysteries of the great classical and modern texts, but the moment her task was terminated, she immediately became impenetrably aloof once more. She never betrayed a single sign of boredom as my teacher, but outside that role she reigned over an unknown territory of forbidden corridors, whence flowed a regular supply of sweets that could not satisfy me.

I have been around the world, locked in a gilded cage. There comes a point in life where one should learn to spread one's wings and fly. I've pretty much passed that point by.

It is too late for the vast horizon of the future.

I am devoted to lead, to sugar, to the earth that will swallow us all.

—

Champs Elysées.

Passage du Lido, with its high opaque glass ceiling. A din like an ocean liner teeming with people. I have embarked on an evening's sugar cruise across a sea of ice cream.

All the desserts on the menu will pass through the critical filter of my digestion. This is the high life, real life, under lights that make copper shine and peach Melba sparkle like glittering enamel. The ecstatic exclamation of a child before the cleverly constructed scaffolding of a multi-colored sorbet sundae.

———

It is useless to try and write when the omelette Norvégienne[5] is so exquisitely prepared.

———

On my way home I see a large woman on the Métro platform. Larger than me, even. My passive, morose twin, resigned to her obesity, to the dress that is now too short, the skirt that rides up her protruding thighs, the shame of non-conformity. And I, satiated, am a little jealous of her size.

Snow in abundance. Winter that actually seems like winter. The chimneys overflow with Chantilly cream. The rooftops have the white sheen of a pudding or a millefeuille[6]. The snow in Parc Monceau crunches under my feet like a perfectly baked meringue. Slothful whiteness as far as the eye can see. Too lazy to go downstairs, to leave the warm shelter of my sugary pit, to stroll down the chestnut cream sidewalks striped with melting snow and sand and salt. Too lazy? Or too scared? I am afraid to face the cold. Contrary to popular belief, the obese are not protected from the chill by their stores of fat. In fact, the thin are better able to withstand extreme changes in temperature. Personally, I would prefer to die of sugar rather than cold.

In any case, I have everything I need to confront the rigors of winter: a lovely wolf-skin coat that Mama tired of and handed down to Zohra. A pointless and grotesque gift, since the poor old Berber would never use such a thing. This Eskimo garb, unknown in her own country, is completely incompatible with her preferred mode of dress. But did my mother even notice? Zohra disposed of it secretly. "Here," she told me recently, "this will make you happy. It smells good."

Actually, the animal scent had not survived the assault of Mama's eau de toilette, except where it lingered under the arms. The lining was stained with faint aureoles of perspiration, and these remnants of slightly stale sweat brought out the fragrance of well-tanned hides. Zohra has a subtle sense of smell, and she knows my own olfactory preferences. She knows I'll never wear the coat, and despite her ample, sprawling curves, I can barely squeeze my own into it.

But I can bury my face in the depths of the fur, sniff the tiniest nooks and crannies of the hide, abandon myself to the thick, soft flamboyance of the pelt.

Those rare times we had to live in cold cities, Mama would throw orgies of fur.

"Fur is my vice," I've heard her say. I came upon her one evening as she showed off her new mink coat to my father. She twirled around like a model, asking him what he thought of it.

"My favorite fur is yours," he replied, kissing her neck. He hadn't even noticed I was there.

13

Other times, going to the opera or the theatre, she
wrapped herself in a big fox-fur stole that still had three
heads attached to it. The glassy little eyes stared evilly at
me.

"Always underfoot!" she cried, seeing me. The mink was
soft and fragrant, and my mother looked fabulous in it.
Needles of ice pierced through her lambskin gloves as she
absently caressed my cheek while checking her make-up
in the hallway mirror.

The memory of beastly flesh, depilated for the splendor of
women, inhaled in blood-soaked nightmares where I am
suffocating under an ice floe. These dreams always chill
me to the bone.

My nose recalls an allergy from one winter in London. I
was wracked by an endless series of sneezes if the tiniest
wisp of animal hair floated by. So Mama forbade me to
come anywhere near her, or to plunge my face into that
wild, silky fur that transformed her into a queen.

At night, I had a pillow filled with synthetic foam,
satisfying her urges toward generosity.

—

What can I do in these polar temperatures besides devote
myself to sugar and write? I spent yesterday under the
covers, munching away at the rest of the cookies. This
morning I went out for a few groceries, but I have no
desire to venture out of my own neighborhood. Classes
barely interest me. They can just wait.

An enormous fruitcake provides an ersatz hearth-fire.
I make it last and last by savoring each ingredient at

length, as others might be absorbed in contemplating the flames of a fireplace. I dissect each slice of the rum-soaked cake one by one with a fingertip, a greedy game of cat and mouse. I extract the morsels of angelica, then the candied cherries, then the raisins, swollen with alcohol. I savor these gems, set into the brown dough, the glory of the English confectioner. When I was in London as a child, I hated currants. By the time we left I liked neither pudding nor cake. According to some immutable, inviolable tradition, they stubbornly persisted in bringing me both of these on a bone china plate every day at five o'clock. No less ceremoniously, the remnants of the cake were returned to the kitchen: with a stroke of my dessert fork, I would produce a freakish ruin on the verge of collapse, riddled with a multitude of grotesque, gaping holes. Then I would build a rampart of crumbs around the edge of the plate. With the raisins I would spell out I DON'T WANT THIS, but in French, so the serving-girl wouldn't understand. This one symbolic act filled me with joy. Today my revolt is far less discreet, but oh, so much sweeter.

———

Maybe I am making a stupid wager with my life. But I know myself. I will go the distance. I shall eat in order to die. After all, they say that there are some people who make love just to die of it.

———

A great discovery today: the indecent, childish pleasure of dipping my fingers into honey, jam, chestnut cream, liquid caramel, fruit yogurt, chocolate sauce, and sucking on them. My fingernails are multi-colored. Mama's carefully manicured hands…the strong, heady odor of her nail polish.

—

So…what it if one day I woke up skinny, or at least thin, or even just a little tubby? What a nightmare! What would become of me without my buoys of flesh, the cocoon of lard that keeps the world at a distance, protecting me from the shock of having to face that world? And how would Mama take it if she suddenly found me her size, and prettier than she (why not?). I suspect that deep down, she prefers me as I am, as much as it does bother her. I could have been a rival, possessed of a velvety gaze, light of step at dances, my lean frame undulating beneath a taffeta gown with a jasmine flower pinned at the neckline. But she has nothing to fear. Nothing.

—

These walls are thin. Next door a boy and a girl hurl insults at each other. Then silence, broken by sobs. Then the rest: breathless little laughs, like the yapping of a dog happy to see its master. The whole time I've lived here I've never encountered any of the other tenants. We're all in the same boat—we spy on one another in order to avoid one another. And yet everyone's story oozes from these indiscreet walls. They don't interest me. They register, but that's all. I just absorb it.

Sometimes their cries put me in a strange state of nervousness. At those moments I will chew, furiously, on anything, no matter what, until the only noises I can hear are the ones coming out of my own mouth.

A Sweet Death

Living like this, amid the disgusting secrets of other people, makes me think I'm right to want to end it all. Or so I tell myself.

—

A flash of realization today: the aerosol can is the supreme invention of the Atomic Age. I have just succumbed to its seductive power. You can get anything in an aerosol can: insecticide, shaving cream, toothpaste, varnish, paint, laundry soap, thermal water, perfume, deodorant…now even crème fraîche comes out of an aerosol can. Chantilly cream at home with the simple push of a button! Sheer magic! Blessed be the gods of progress, the guardian angels of gourmands, the patron saints of those afflicted with a sweet tooth!

The gadget does have its charms. I bought one this morning and tried it immediately. The cream spurts out of a star-shaped opening in the spout in an elaborate jet. Yes, ladies, now you can easily add a touch of whimsy to your desserts: arabesques, stucco-like texturing, pompadour curls, Himalayan snows or Gothic lettering. The anonymous housewife is elevated to the dignified rank of Artiste while standing between her dishwasher and her microwave oven. Personally, I couldn't care less about aesthetics.

The instructions specifically say to hold the can vertically over the tart, ice cream or fruit. I, however, want the cream directly in my mouth. I start to get a cramp in my neck from straining to lean my head back far enough to fill myself up with this wondrous stuff. A substance so light you'd think you were swallowing an illusion.

It doesn't occur to me to simply lie down. By the time
I finally do think of it, I barely have enough left to
decorate my lips with a lacy ruffle of cream. To renew this
ephemeral pleasure, I go out and brave the cold to buy
three more cans. The urgency of my greed overcomes the
dreadful prospect of having to climb back up seven flights
of stairs.

And then, I abandon myself to delight. Stretched
out comfortably on the bed, holding the can straight
overhead, my finger pressing slowly on the trigger of
pleasure, I watch the long, foamy vanilla serpent spring
from the plastic nozzle and coil itself into the oblivion of
my wide-open maw.

Now I take my time, battling my gluttonous impatience,
savoring this delicious, self-inflicted force-feeding,
muzzling myself with a gag of sugar.

Then nothing but four empty, useless cans—impossible to
refill, cumbersome symbols of a world in which everything
is disposable.

I shake each one furiously, with all my strength. I inhale,
sucking at the nozzles as best as I can to extract the last
traces of cream. A sugary gas and a few deliquescent
morsels are all I can achieve.

Disappointed at finishing them, I toss the exhausted cans
on the floor. I long to squash them under the steamroller
of my body, to flatten them and roll them out like tubes of
toothpaste, squeezing out every last tidbit of enchantment.
Exasperated, I fall asleep. I am now emerging from a
clammy slumber, writing these words with a foul taste
upon my tongue. I am impatient for daybreak: as soon as

the shops are open I can quench this irrepressible desire for those aerosol cans. It is an urge that torments me, keeping me awake.

———

I shall die of indigestion, warm under my rolls of fat. Happy.

———

A telegram informs me of my parents' imminent departure for Madagascar. Mama begs me to show some sign of life, and soon. The telegram is her way of showing her disapproval of my living here, without comforts, without my own running water, without a telephone, like a student completely bereft of any financial support. For me to live in these servants' quarters, when they could so easily afford to offer me a studio, is beneath my "social position".

"Well, if this is what you really want, then it's up to you!"

Up to me, indeed. She wouldn't come here to visit even if her life depended on it. Slogging up the service stairs in couture? Such inconvenience…

And thus, my tranquility is guaranteed. These twenty square meters under the eaves, on the seventh floor of a working-class building—my little nest, a snug shell up above Paris, above the world, above that golden sphere where my mother evolved. But suppose she had a serious reason to come here? I could pick her knock from out of a thousand: a smart, light tap so she doesn't chip her nail polish. Given the general state of disorder in here, I would quickly throw a sheet over my stash of sweets before opening the door. She would be shocked, of course, by the scanty space, the lack of both light and charm, the poverty of my scattered clothing, and, above all, the stagnant reek of pigeon shit that no amount of airing has ever been able to dissipate.

She couldn't possibly imagine that I am sacrificing everything to sugar: space, comfort, everyday amusements, elegance. But sugar is worth all these things—and more—to someone who has decided to die of it.

—

The Student returned those notes I loaned him. He asked which high school I had attended. I have no intention of telling him my life story. My life? What a joke. And a tasteless one at that. I simply told him that I had studied for the baccalaureate exam with a private tutor. As for the rest, I kept my mouth shut. The concrete facts that describe my brief existence do not coincide with my shocking image. I am a big fat fraud. My less-than-sprightly gait and immovable bulk make people see me as completely sedentary. Who would ever believe in my still-recent peregrinations as the daughter of a diplomat? They already detect a degree of artifice in my literary abilities, my aesthetic sensibilities, my intellectual ease—so out of place in such an awkward and ungainly body. Don't they?

Who would believe me? The Student no more than anybody else. Besides, it's impossible to prove. I can remember nothing of these trips, except the names of cities where I wasn't even allowed to go sight-seeing. I learned nothing of local customs. The exotic sweets? I

recall only an uncontrollable revulsion towards cakes
I didn't even want to taste. I can remember flashes
of fragrant colors in the landscapes, and the clinging
sensation of always being adrift. Mama always kept me
apart from other children, whether French or native.
I know nothing of the world beyond the impersonal
luxury of consular residences: the lengthy unrolling of
red carpets in deserted corridors, the gleam of polished
floors, the unfathomable depths of huge mirrors showing
endlessly reflected rooms. I have never breathed in the
dust of schoolroom classes, nor torn my smock during the
effervescent hours of recess. I have never taken a turn at
hopscotch, never leapt into that space between heaven
and earth. Eternally absent from the uproars, the hall
patrols, the small joys, the copying of lines. I dreamed
up austere boarding schools for myself, rumbling with
whispers and nocturnal conspiracies. In those gilded
salons I was initiated into the solitude of the only child,
establishing imaginary complicities, hatching schemes to
run away or play truant, along with dormitory rebellions
that never materialized.

I was intoxicated by the idea of prisons and promiscuity,
of dry bread and broom closets. Poor kids probably
dream of the snug, dainty world I inhabited as a "model
child". But a sharp eye would have seen in that model
child an unwillingness to smile, a propensity for frowning,
a refusal to believe all the rubbish that grown-ups always
tell kids…so many signposts of an unflinching sense of
determination.

—

I end up having to go to her.

Her sharp look is ferocious beneath her long, mascara-ed lashes. She judges my rotundity with a single glance. To all evidence, I have put on still more weight. But at the table, I barely pick at my food. She sees that plainly. When the coffee arrives, she hands me the card of a doctor friend of hers.

"He's a trustworthy man. He'll have you looking presentable by the time we get back from Madagascar."

Her unexpected words sound like a death knell amid the clatter of coffee spoons. My father agrees absently. It's amazing he's even here, really.

I think she's more concerned with the perfidious clucking of gossip regarding my health than she is about my actual health.

———

They are leaving for a year. Little by little, I am losing my sense of time. Does she honestly think that's enough time for me to relinquish the perfect dimensions of a sphere?

Of course, she won't pass up a single opportunity to pop back up to Paris. She'll say it with a false nonchalance— she needs to stock up on perfume and cosmetics. No matter where they send my father she always says, "It is a country where one cannot find anything."

Will she keep me in the loop about these return trips to France? Or will she reserve those visits exclusively for her small coterie of faithful friends? Or perhaps lovers? Even in the alcoholic languor of tropical evenings, will she maintain her preoccupation with my uncanny resemblance to a dirigible?

A Sweet Death

She hasn't suggested that I go and stay in Boulevard
Suffet during their absence. Will it make her impromptu
return visits easier? In illicit company, perhaps? But
anyway, she knows I would refuse to abandon my lair.

—

This time I take advantage of the bathroom. In the giant
mauve tub, my bloated stomach floats to the surface of
the water, gleaming like sealskin, smooth and distended,
piled rolls of fat between my breasts and groin.

Inside, known only to me, is a muddle of entrails
encrusted with sugar. And beneath all that, ovaries the
size of grapefruits, no doubt, keeping up with the rest of
me. I have nothing else but a skeleton buried under this
proliferation of greasy flesh.

All of this is mine.

But am I really the mistress of my cells' future? I grasp my
waist. I see my breasts conquer new territory, out into the
void, pushing their limits, unstoppable.

All of this is mine, this warm softness surrounding me. But
no—nothing really belongs to me except the freedom to
separate myself forever from this swollen, worthless sack
of gas, water and fat, whenever I choose to do so.

—

In one year, in this very same mauve temple, where
the rituals of maternal beauty are cultivated and
perpetuated, shall lie my corpse: a cracked, mottled
iceberg; a discolored marble by Maillol[7], preserved in the
sugar-saturated bathwater. Thighs stuck together. Arms

welded to breasts, and breasts glued together. Fingers indistinguishable from the puffy mass of my shapeless hands.

—

I will hold on until I am too full of myself.

—

For now, though, I don't find myself quite horrible enough just yet.

—

But I am forgetting the essential point, which I discovered after my bath. The door to her bedroom wasn't shut. And then came the temptation to pilfer a morsel of her privacy: peeking at the gems in her jewelry box, looking into her half-open purse, a glimpse of the lingerie she left hanging on the back of a chair. I went in. Everything was in order. The housekeeper had acquitted herself of her tasks perfectly, leaving nothing out of place. On the nightstand lay the Pléiade edition of the complete works of Baudelaire[3], a green bookmark about two-thirds of the way through. Ah, the mysteries of my mother's choices in reading material. My heart was pounding. Delight in indiscretion. Where exactly was she in the book? I waited to open it, trying to guess first, to keep the surprise in check. Baudelaire suits her. A languid odalisque, glittering with jewels, freely offering the splendor of her nakedness. She delights in some venomous poem or other while awaiting the veneration, the caresses of her master.

We had read *Les fleurs du mal* together. The commentary I wrote about it scored an exceptionally high grade on my baccalaureate exam. Poems learned by heart, which she had trained me to recite back. Suspended breath, crackling consonants, smooth vowels, words rolling around on the tongue, soft murmurs, the rhythm of silences and refined musicality. The sober pleasure of indulging in an emotional drama. She transformed into a magnificent actress in the blink of an eye. I drank in the vermillion perfume of her voice, and I couldn't have said which enchanted me more: the poetry or my mother.

She was at the chapter "Of Women and Girls". Here Baudelaire evokes "the roundness of fat, that hideous health and idleness."

My eyes went straight to those words in the middle of the page. I read nothing else.

No comment.

—

Yesterday I refused all commentary.

Today I protest. Not against Baudelaire but against her, as she shares, then appropriates, the thoughts of the poet in judgment of me. I protest against the accusation of "idleness." Does my mother have any idea how much work is required to create this corpulence? The perseverance of an ant, exhausting errands, small physical violences. Me, idle? The huntress of bonbons, detective of rare pastries, engulfer of sweets, the implacable devourer?

Of course, I'll lose my health. But I will gain in hideousness. And that shall be my recompense.

—

They are there, south of the equator. Without me. How does that change things for my father? Engrossed almost entirely in his duties, and otherwise preoccupied almost exclusively with my mother, he has barely ever done more than run across me by sheer chance. I have no idea why he's even stayed in Paris these past few months. But then, the finer points of diplomacy have always escaped me. He left France in top form, impatient for this new and distant exile. As for Mama, all her time belongs to him anyway. Finished are the lessons she continued to give me, "for fear that student life will make you a complete idiot". Finished are the clandestine fitting sessions in her room, intended to turn me into a less unpalatable creature. Her maternal obligations are fulfilled. Soon she will be back in the nearly cinematographic ostentation of grand ambassadorial soirées. She will float like a butterfly, a queen, an incomparable beauty with scorched wings. She will be rid of me. And I of her. Rid of her, yes, but deprived of the indispensable Zohra, upon whom the mindless phobia of airplanes has been inflicted one more time.

Zohra has taken flight. She has been stolen from me. Zohra, who, for the first time in her life, has fooled herself into the naïve belief that we will see each other again soon. The too-confident Zohra will suppress her instincts, which are those of a faithful old beast able to scent my death from the other side of the globe. My tiny, wrinkled Zohra, lost in her over-laundered skirts and petticoats. My weary little weasel, eyes heavy with secrets. Ancient hands, perfumed neck. My loyal, tender old accomplice with the inscrutable smile.

—

I won't be following them any longer. I am now forever fixed at the same meridian.

—

Curious. The Student is becoming interested in me. It is crucial that he be discouraged. Each of his questions is a small act of aggression, a subtle invasion into my closed universe. The blanket of cellulite that insulates me from the rest of the world must be placed between him and me as well. I am much too used to my own company to accept his disruption of my tranquil silence.

He wants to read my work—all of it, in its entirety. He wants to know my theories about this author, that book. He wants to make the clever monkey speak. So be it. So what if he finds out that my thoughts consist of nothing but honey and caramel, ink on paper like jam spread upon a slice of bread?

—

I'll invite him to La Gourmandise. He'll drink some coffee and smoke some of those pale, reeking American cigarettes. The stunning spectacle of my bulimic prowess will parade before him: profiteroles[9], banana splits drowning in whipped cream, spongy Moka[10], religieuses au chocolat[11], lemon tarts, babas au rhum[12], congolais[13], chaussons napolitains[14], têtes de nègre[15]. I will not refuse a single cake if it helps me protect my solitude and my secrecy.

—

I will nauseate him, to the point of disgusting him with my very words.

If I speak to him, it will be with my mouth full.

—

A tea-room, rue de Rivoli.

They are accustomed to my presence here now. As the best customer in the establishment, I have earned the right to a few considerations. They graciously offer me a chocolate liqueur or suggest a new menu item for my appraisal. They have designated a table just for me, where I can sit undisturbed and write in my little notebook. I carry it with me everywhere now.

I spend a lot of afternoons in this quiet oasis of elegant gluttony.

How long the afternoons can be. Mama used to leave me alone with an essay topic. As long as she was still there, as long as I could still hear her humming as she prepared to go out, I could not concentrate. Her light, silky step, the trail of her perfume, her dry evasive kiss from afar, from the tips of painted lips that never actually touched my face. A taxi waited. She had no more time. I must save myself. She has saved herself. The fairy has flown. She never said where she was going. To tea-rooms like this one? Boudoirs? Beds?

Then I worked without any difficulty. When the essay was done I would place it on her vanity table so she would find it when she came in to take off her make-up. Sometimes it would be very late. Sometimes it would even be the wee hours of the morning.

When I awoke I would find little packages on my nightstand, parcels festooned with curling ribbons and the gilded tag of some famous confectioner. Petit-fours, high quality chocolates, filled bonbons, always the same type of thing. I doubt she had the time to choose them herself, just as she never had time to make sure I was actually asleep before leaving on the table beside the bed.

Well, I wasn't sleeping. I've always been a very light sleeper. And my memory is heavy with so many sweets never tasted but secretly dumped in the huge garbage bin in the kitchen.

One day, before they went out, she lifted my chin with her gloved hand and said, "So, my child—when are you going to decide to be pretty?" The next morning I found nothing on the nightstand.

She hadn't had the time.

—

Jardin de Luxembourg. I am experiencing the effort of walking. Slow steps and a belly heavy with apple fritters dusted with granulated sugar. The pond is frozen over so the remote-controlled boats are impossible to navigate. Perfect little boys and perfect little girls, dolls all got up in wool, cheeks full of roasted chestnuts. They think: "Look at the fat lady! The happy snow-woman! The statue carved out of lard!" I pass through the middle of their laughter. Then, out of sight, out of mind. They go back to their games, their bickering, their snowball fights. Have I ever even touched snow with my bare hands? Just a fingertip once, in London. Just enough to know how much it burns. But the racket of these battles? Never. It's mostly been violent rain and tropical humidity. Like they have in Madagascar, where I will never go.

On the beach, or next to a private swimming pool, Mama's friends display their gleaming skins. Lean and bronzed, plucked down to their toenails, stinking of amber musk. The puny little buttons of their desiccated breasts poke from beneath minuscule triangles of satiny fabric, paid for dearly in some boutique in the rue Saint-Honoré. They strike mermaid poses on a close-cropped lawn without a single blade of grass out of place. A lawn as smooth as a shaved armpit. I would crush that green carpet under my buttocks. My breasts would ooze liquefied gelatin from all sides. Rivulets of translucent jam—raspberry, or maybe cherry sweat, the product of my hard-working cells—flow from under my arms. The sun penetrates the milky husk of my deathly pale skin. A multitude of sizzling fatty curds, a melting, seething mass of bubbles burst under my skin. I would be delighted by the horrified looks on those ladies' faces. They would wonder whence sprang this fried and broiled gargoyle, its body like an agonized beast doing somersaults. I would need to gasp laboriously upon standing up again. I would plunge into the turquoise pool, the oily stains of my melting body soiling the serene blue of the water's surface.

—

Why do I get such a delight from horror?

—

Sometimes I want to lick the brown bodies of the women on magazine covers until I swoon. Instead I buy caramel lollipops.

—

Memories float to the surface of my mind, entirely at the mercy of my nibblings. The year I took the baccaluareate exam. The end of my tête-à-têtes with my Mama, struggling with an academic load too heavy for the two hours a day she devoted to my studies. She had the necessary education to take me farther herself, but not the time. I fell behind, they waited, I got myself together again and caught back up. Then the beauty queen disappeared again in a cloud of powder and fur, accompanying my father on a new assignment. They enrolled me in a private school.

At the age of seventeen, my fellow pupils—though not my peers—were unveiled to the world in the effervescence of their first amorous adventures. They were slender. They prattled on about the meeting of lips. Supple waists, flat stomachs. Sparkling with gaiety, delighting in romantic chagrin. They rustled about, measuring their hips, comparing themselves to each other, trading fashion magazines and reading lists. They said the baccalaureate wasn't good for anything, as they piled iridescent shadow onto their eyelids, cordially detesting one another until they reconciled amidst mad laughter, whispers, giggles, secrets.

Some had an almost maternal fullness to their bodies, self-assured as the figurehead on a ship's prow. My nose was buried in a book but my ears were open as I shrouded myself in silence. Everything about them frightened me. Initiation into the world. Did I really have to try and be like them? To learn how to talk and dance and smile? To be a languid cooing girl abandoning myself to the weight of a man, under a window? Mama played a waltz on the piano while the guests hummed a quiet counterpoint to the music, heavy with heat and alcohol. Trapped in an existence wherein they believed me to be fast asleep, but all the while I was carefully measuring each nuance of the masquerade. My eyes were trained upon the world, and I learned hypocrisy. I refused to smile.

The aviary opened. Wings beat and fluttered. Schoolgirls enjoying themselves out in the cafés.

The boys from the high school across the street waited for them, to talk about Baudelaire, Kierkegaard[16], Rimbaud[17], the latest hot album. The baccalaureate exam. A farce, a joke, the boys bragged. The girls were festive, flowery. Me, I was on the other side—a dried thistle, an albatross without wings. I wasn't quite so fat at that point. Just ugly. Ugly by absence. Extinguished. Neutered. Nothing passed my way—neither interest nor boredom. It was the smile that was missing. "Why bother putting on lipstick if you aren't going to smile?"

Mama was right. Anyway, I've never bothered trying to paint my lips. Smiling is beyond my capabilities. I'd do pretty well in a wax museum.

And then—sugar. Little bits at first. Some gum, a bonbon, a chocolate, while reading philosophy at boarding school. I would mechanically buy my own little parcels to put on the nightstand. Mama was almost certainly dying of the heat in Dakar then. Long meditations on death, on the meaning of life, all swirling together. And then the seed of an idea, confused at first. Then clearer. To die by sugar, my mouth full of sugar. To do things differently from everyone else. The other girls tracked the progression of my corpulence with sidelong glances. The results? Brilliant. I intrigued them a little. But none of them sought my company. Well, the feeling was mutual.

My diploma in hand, I weighed in at eighty kilos. Eighty was the goal for the start of my university career. After all the empty years spent in huge, deserted apartments, I plunged headlong into my own generation. The boys, my brethren, were no surprise. Sitting next to them in lecture halls, I could sense which ones embodied the future of the consular soirée. They tottered between the serious and the careless, between indefatigable work and blatant idleness, between conformity and laborious originality. Most of them already had an incurable case of verbal diarrhea. They amused me some, but more often than not I found them tiresome, even though they never actually addressed a single word to me.

These girls, these boys…I have nothing to say to them. They are all lost in the relentless pursuit of games and seductions. The only prospects they have are cowardice, break-ups and betrayal.

—

So old already. Well, luckily I still have most of a that marble cake and a whole package of sweet prunes.

—

Tonight, here I am, forced to use a ballpoint pen. I despise this particular species of writing utensil. My fountain pen broke when it fell on the floor. The nib is completely mangled. I tried fixing it but it's no good. It is unusable.

Words are coming to me with difficulty, doubtless because of this cold ink that leaves nothing but dry scratchings. The meager script is so sad, such a contrast to the well-fed, woolly rounds of the preceding pages. My writing doesn't resemble me today. My gaze flutters about, as if trying to escape the image of another possible form I might take: the thin fragile traces left by this ballpoint.

In another life, perhaps—former or future—my body had, or will have, the evanescent lightness of this pale ink. Even the paper doesn't want to drink it in.

I interrupt myself frequently. I go back, page by page, to retrace the thick current of my almost daily interior monologues, which have been consigned to this notebook ever since a certain, deliberately omitted, date.

I scoff at my own obstinacy in trying to extract such a detailed catalogue of vague memories and gustatory sensations from the void of my existence.

I forge ahead, toward that empty nothingness, through an underbrush of words, delighting in the endless meandering and sheer uselessness of….everything.

And yet, this evening I really do miss the syrupy flow of that licorice ink; the ephemeral gleam of black liquid, slow to dry in the curve of a vowel, the point of an accent, the end of the crossing of a T. Tomorrow, even before my mouth gets its ration of sugar, I am going to treat myself to a lovely new Waterman with a well-wrought nib.

The floor is stained with black blotches, indelible blemishes mapping the course of the ruined pen as it fell. There are starfish and buttons, Chinese characters and cuneiform script, dots, double hooks, bushy eyebrows, those little round beauty spots you stick to your cheekbones at Carnival time, and, rather disturbingly, an entire faun looming over a cluster of bizarre-looking ants and some other hairy insects.

This is what I have discovered just now, examining the stained floor from up close. I spent a long time absorbed in deciphering these arcane symbols, ballpoint between my teeth and respiration nearly cut off from being down on all fours so I could see better. Getting back up on my feet took a great deal of effort. Suffocation. My blood is no longer circulating. Dizziness. My plan for achieving the systematic malfunction of my corporeal machine is starting to demonstrate some appreciable results.

I have just used the last of my strength trying to get the congealed ink to come out of this damn pen. I'm counting to two, and then it's going to find itself in a trash bin!

—

I am writing this with a peppy new fountain pen! What a pleasure to rediscover these ebony words, fleshy words drawn with lovely, thick, oily ink! In the end, I renounced the too-classic Waterman, seduced by the new Shaeffer model. It's a beautiful streamlined instrument of swimming-pool blue Bakelite, translucent as a sourball. I can see the level of the ink cartridge go down without having to take the whole thing apart. A new era is dawning, founded upon my resolution not to chew on the caps of my pen. I had the distressing habit of doing that with that last Waterman. So now I am writing with pen in hand and a caramel in my mouth.

———

When I woke up this morning the caramel still hadn't dissolved completely. I had tucked it into the corner of my cheek for the night, wedged it in there with my raspy tongue. Experiencing the taste of sugar at the moment of waking has no rival for dispelling the pressing weight of tormented dreams. I generally don't dream much, or least I don't remember specific images that stream across the canvas of my sleeping mind. But last night was just the opposite. I clearly saw enormous ink stains assaulting me from all sides: giant animals from another time—half-insect, half-fish creatures unleashed and emerging from a primordial ocean, cold as ice. I did not resist. I offered myself to them, docile, acquiescing to the peril that assailed me. I felt I had to disappear from this world and its ways for all eternity. Soon nothing remained of my bodily husk, or of my attackers, or of the tempest. I had become the consciousness of the sea.

At that point someone slammed the door to the landing. It was then that my tongue found the caramel.

———

The time will come when I shall be the consciousness of sugar.

—

I don't feel like writing today.

—

Things to say. No strength to say them.

—

Another empty page today too.

—

I am obsessed with the stains on the floor. I eat. The
Student hasn't been in class. And I haven't been to La
Gourmandise. I will go later, with him. If he wants.

—

Since I had that dream, I am totally engrossed with those
splotches of ink. One in particular attracts me. Digestion
leads to a sort of semi-hypnotic state in which this stain
invariably takes the shape of a scorpion with a curved tail.
Sometimes I stare at it for so long that it shrinks to a tiny
point no bigger than the head of a pin. My eyes blur with
stinging tears. Then a terrible migraine pulverizes my
skull.

—

The scorpion haunts me. It's almost like he has it in for
me. Like he wants me to just shut up and be quiet.

—

I attend class assiduously. The Student still hasn't come
back. Could he be ill? Or on a trip?

—

Studying is now useless to me except as a distraction from the ink stain. In the muffled atmosphere of the library, I amuse myself by watching all these eager-beaver students at work while I munch on a candy bar.

—

The melted sugar of the tarte Tatin[18] releases a gentle puff of steam, perfumed with hot apples. It sticks to my silver fork and I diligently suck it from each tine, one by one. Outside, lashing sheets of rain fling themselves at Paris, mixed with tiny hailstones that clatter against the cars. Outside is a hostile jungle under a monsoon sky. I am fine, warm in the hollow of my seat, having only to issue the command for a succulent slice of the Mademoiselles Tatin's[19] creation to be slid in front of me. I imagine those women—conspirators of greedy, hungry children everywhere—as very old and very charming. I see them in the kitchen, their pointed expert noses sniffing out the treasures of the oven. Measuring a pinch of sugar, their fingers demonstrate the sureness of long experience. They whisper pastry secrets to each other, lips trembling in the anticipated pleasure of a universally appreciated dessert, the success of which has retained a hidden dose of both malice and tenderness.

Outside it is forever water, water, water—a flood from which I shall be the only happy escapee.

A gray mist quickly covers the windows of the tea-room, effectively pulling a curtain across the outside world. I am in the sweet, warm softness of tarts and chocolate. The

Mlles Tatin are keeping an eye on me. The exterior world no longer exists.

—

How I hope Eternity is just like this.

—

A lull in the storm.

—

Despite being forbidden to "go down" to the kitchens (though we would "go down" all the time when we needed to see the domestic staff), boredom would occasionally lead me there. Satiated with literature, I could no longer concentrate. The apartments were too vast and the gardens too sad, probably because they were so lovely yet so empty.

I needed a living soul.

Very sensitive to the eaux de toilette that Mama used, I had a sufficiently subtle nose to differentiate between the heady perfumes and exotic oils that the native women smoothed onto their bodies. I could pick them out among the strong odors of spices, yeast, fried onions, grilled peppers, poached fish, orange blossom water and dirty dishes. As much as I detested sweets back then, I hungered for these fragrances. I would have bitten down willingly upon amber and musk had there been bonbons made from their scents.

They would offer me some fruit, a pastry, an orange soda. I would always decline. To make up for it, the elderly Zohra would offer up her wrinkled neck to me, replete with a bouquet of odors both mild and acid: a mysterious blend of henna, cloves and citronella, a mixture to which only she knew the secret. A maddened animal, lost to sense, I buried my nose in her neck and inhaled until my lungs were ready to burst. I didn't speak. It was good. It was sweet.

Nowadays, tartes Tatin have the same effect on me.

—

I threw out that fur coat.

It will be a gift to the first passer-by who comes across it. Some shrewd night-owl will find it on top of the big plastic garbage can that the concierge puts out down in the alley.

Berating the shameful profligacy of the rich, he will nevertheless be thrilled to take full advantage of that same wastefulness and will stoop down to pick it up. With its high-quality tanning and its luster, and still looking like new, that coat will be the joy of whatever woman he gives it to.

From here on out, there will be nothing more in my room. No other odors but my own.

—

A sleepless night. No provisions. I ate everything before midnight, not foreseeing this intractable insomnia. There are a few traces of solidified jelly in an otherwise empty jar. I swipe them out with a fingertip. I suck on my index finger for a long time, imagining the taste of blueberries. This makes me drool heavily. I could tell myself that I'm

eating pound cakes overflowing with honey and cream,
stealing them from a pastry shop's display case while
the baker is turned away to his oven or concocting some
sugary invention, kneading his dough or stewing his fruit
compotes, adding in the vanilla and cinnamon. I could
name all the delicious things I've eaten from memory, all
night long, without even peeking in my notebook. I could
satisfy myself with imaginary chocolates the color of ink
and quadrille paper. Gorge myself on juicy, exotic words:
guava, touron[20], halvah, loukoum[21], cornes de gazelle[22]…
but writing about this insufferable dearth will do nothing
to ease it.

———

I will go out into the darkness. Down to that all-night
drugstore by the Opéra. I will order all of their leftover
tarts and chocolate mousse. I will sit down in front a
sundae wreathed in Chantilly cream and I will make it
last as long as possible.

———

How many moves are required to get there? At this late
hour there are no buses, and the Métro isn't running.
The taxi station is about a five-minute walk from here.
It's an icy itinerary through empty streets. My shadow
precedes me from one streetlamp to the next, huge
and abominable. An alley-cat emerges from a recessed
doorway and slinks between my legs, just like in a scene at
the movies. I can hear pop music coming from a taxi. As I
draw near, I realize that the radio is poorly tuned and that
the driver is napping, his head on the steering wheel.

"To the Opéra drugstore, please!"

The man jumps and excuses himself out of habit, turning the key in the ignition with a sleepy gesture. He asks me to repeat my destination and sneaks a glance in the rear-view mirror. Seeing the monster, he believes himself plunged back into the disturbing landscape of his interrupted nightmare — perhaps a land of giant trees and muddy rivers where enormous naked women suffocate infants by the thousands between their flabby teats. Far off in the distance, the sea is the dirty white of burnt milk. The taxi is slowly sucked into the maw of a whirling vortex. The driver witnesses the destruction of his vehicle, powerless. He ponders the Herculean strength of those women, who could have saved his car with a single gesture. But no one cares about him, and he too will be swallowed by the vortex soon enough.

I intervene in time to keep him from slipping back into sleep. I want to tell him that no, I do not belong to that race of ogresses, that he has nothing to fear from me, that I just want a sweet little snack to help me get to sleep. I would move the entire city of Paris just to put a morsel of sugar under my tongue. What's so strange about that? A smoker would do the same thing for a pack of cigarettes.

—

I could sit here all night long, indulging in these flights of imagination. But they won't satisfy my cravings.

—

In the end, my nocturnal foray presented no difficulties whatsoever. All I had to do was obey the orders of my impatient, salivating mouth. Another taxi neatly deposited two men at the end of my block, people I didn't know, but who must have seen the little troll from number 7. I heard their bursts of laughter, an effeminate laughter, very high-pitched. As I was getting into the car, I heard one of them way, "My word! She's a refugee from a Diane Arbus[23] exhibit!" The other one laughed even harder. Then it struck me that that they were laughing at me. I have no idea who Diane Arbus is. A cartoonist, no doubt. I'll look into it for myself when I get the chance.

I enjoy quite a feast at the drugstore despite the reddish lights that distort the color of the cakes. I load myself up as best as I can with crème caramel[24] and piping hot tarte Tatin. A display of exotic items is presented among a pile of pretty blue boxes. Metal boxes, round and heavy, with a colorful, primitive image from "The Thousand and One Nights" on the lid—halvah! I was just dreaming about it less than an hour ago in the pages of this very notebook. It is said that to name a thing is to bring into being. Perhaps. Will death come more quickly if I write its name each day in careful, rounded letters?

———

Eaten in sufficient quantities, halvah proves itself to be marvelously indigestible. This greasy, dense substance has imparted upon my silhouette the Oriental curves of a new Scheherazade. My breasts are growing under muslin veils, heavy with Turkish tidbits and Persian sweetmeats that would make the sultans convulse in delight.

Claude Tardat

—

Perched on a cafeteria stool, I watch the endless line of students. I have decided not to do any more work this afternoon.

I think I can safely say that I am the most advanced specimen of obesity in the entire university. The boys tend more toward thinness and suppressed nervousness; among some of the more devout militants—political, labor, or religious—it goes nearly to the point of emaciation. Books and newspapers replace food, and it is intellectual chatter that stimulates their salivary glands. One might say they have big heads, but the rest of them certainly hasn't followed suit. Puny shrimps with sunken shoulders, now stiff, now agile, moving through crowds, always exalted, always sure of their appearance, always in a hurry to launch into debates or monologues. They gobble up their sandwiches mechanically, without ever noticing what's in them. Their coffees go cold between their critique of a new film and their political commentary on current events. The indispensable cigarette, a basic accessory for any and all discussions, consumes itself between the speaker's fingertips. They never notice, too absorbed in showering their listener—female by preference—with the latest linguistic theories they've learned. In professorial tones, they explain what they believe you never could have grasped without their help. They usually punctuate their sentences by stabbing out their cigarettes in an ashtray already overflowing with butts.

But where can The Student possibly be?

The girls aren't really fat either. Plump once in a while, or maybe well-built and solid in a sporty kind of way, they're too busy preparing for exams and keeping in shape to indulge in those excesses of pastry in which I so often luxuriate. But they do nibble; staggered snacks that they allow themselves between study sessions at the library or literature classes. A chocolaty pause…but it is all calibrated by some precise schedule in which the quantity of candy consumed is a function of the cerebral energy that was just expended.

I hear talk of tennis, rowing, dance, yoga, wind-surfing. It is a sign that even here, in this ivory tower, where ideas are shuffled and scattered about like playing cards, that we have still not forsaken the fleshly body. The whole body. The body modeled after ancient ideals of beauty, the body displayed in perfect plasticity. The body that Mama tried so very hard to engineer for me, with private lessons in gymnastics and classical dance that one of her friends agreed to provide out of affection for her. I will never have that disciplined, well-toned body. That pretend body. That illusory body. Mama's body.

But what's so great about that other body?

Oh, how irritating they all are, and tiresome their prattling! What am I doing here among them? I have nothing to learn here. Their obliviousness, their seriousness, their frivolity—laughable. I want to slice open my belly with a single stroke, like the generous pelican, so they will all run screaming from the nauseating wave of my entrails. I'll throw in the satin slippers Mama bought when I was learning toe dancing and leaps. And the inevitable pink candy-floss tutu, fluffed like the crest of an egret. Nowadays I'd barely be able to get it half-way down my forehead. I would offer myself up, fodder for their endless gossip, revealing the fatal path of study, dance, sports and sugar.

——

I saw The Student again yesterday as I was getting ready to leave the cafeteria. He left a small group of people in the middle of an animated conversation to come over and say hello, and to ask what's new.

"We should meet someplace besides here," he suggested.

So I invited him to La Gourmandise, where he shall see what he shall see.

——

Mistake. Diane Arbus isn't a cartoonist. According to The Student, she's an American photographer who is famous for her portraits of giants, dwarfs and other carnival sideshow freaks. So that man the other night was actually doing me an honor, associating me with those "Largest Women In The World" who get exhibited by shady, opportunistic Barnum types, and whom, it seems, Diane Arbus spent her life hunting in seedy lairs.

——

Information to verify. Find those photos.

——

Zohra used to tell me African legends. One of them was about a scorpion. I forget how it goes. The ink stain is just as black as ever.

A Sweet Death

———

From the room next door, I hear cascades of girlish laughter, punctuated with panting and heavy sighs. They're giving me the gift of a soundtrack, but I'm left to reconstruct the images of the film.

Some nights the neighbor girl is overcome with anger, and her shrill voice makes our dividing wall tremble. A man is with her. He knocked on her door an hour ago. She opened it. They talked. Then laughter. Now he's silent, undoubtedly powerless to keep her verbal storm in check. Unless, of course, he's actually enjoying the progression of the spectacle.

I don't really care about her life, but sometimes it is thrust upon me, heavy with the weight of noise and indiscretions. In these moments, all I can do is inhale some sweetened condensed milk. I close my eyes, a straw in my mouth, letting the thick cream flow. Do they hear the sucking sound when I get to the end of it? Mainly I just want to shield my ears from her hysterical yapping.

———

In a confusion of cries, Mama is howling. A long time ago. A tunnel.

Or maybe I just dreamed it?

———

At La Gourmandise, this afternoon.

Is The Student a practitioner of the worldly art of complacency? Not the slightest flicker of surprise toward

me. Not the least manifestation of disgust or impatience
with my ingestional capabilities. No fishy story to flee
my presence as quickly as possible. Quite the opposite—
we spent two hours talking. He seems fascinated by
my babblings about Russian literature between bites
of millefeuille. I drool over the pastry, and he drools in
admiration over the extent of my cultural education.
Where had I found the time, at such a young age, to read
all those epics? He is repelled by their length. Passion,
I reply evasively, without clarifying that this passion
is now sterile, replaced with a passion for sugar. I am
reciting things at him, like rote lessons that have no real
importance, giving opinions about authors I no longer
care anything about. I hold forth, as everyone does in
school, but I don't get worked up. I maintain my distance,
remaining calm. This gives me an air of gravity, of
wisdom.

Dostoïevski[25]. Tolstoï[26]. Bulgakov[27]. My nights are
crammed with pages, cluttered with memories. I'm an
overweight, flabby seagull. Tchekhov[28], a long time
ago on a somewhat foggy evening in London. I had no
friends and no visitors, so I swallowed the words and spit
the best ones back out. It was no longer me speaking,
but some stranger who had appropriated my voice to
parrot things that any idiot could say. The banality of
those words shouldn't fool anyone. Conversations must
be fed: foul broth, chopped meat, crumbs, all mashed
up with the Russian authors and their great souls. I can't
do it anymore. I am in the sugar-laden here and now,
with tartlets lined up upon my plate. Nothing is more
important than the immediacy of these fleshy cherries,
these plums and apricots. I can talk to him about books

for hours if that's what he wants, but my own priority is to eat, eat the whole time. As long as I can speak, I will eat: never sated, never quite full.

Then a sudden, slicing blow, like the cut of a scalpel: "Why do you hide yourself?"

I can prove The Student wrong—this has been a day of non-stop exhibitionism. Granted, it has been indoors where it's warm. It's rather chilly out today.

—

"Look, Mommy! The fat lady is going to tip the bus over!" exclaimed a little girl with huge, astonished eyes when I boarded the 138 at random. Her neck craning, she was proudly enthroned in her seat, her little legs dangling into the void, too short to reach the floor. Patent leather shoes, clean socks, Sunday-best frock, impeccable bangs. The model of a polite, well-mannered child who has just committed an utterly naïve blunder. I felt sorry for her. Next to the girl, the mother kept her nose stuck to the window and stayed silent, as if she had heard nothing.

The "lady"—me—didn't deserve such a title. I laughed heartily, quite loudly, and the little girl began to laugh with me, reassured that my unusual size wasn't going to keep the bus from continuing its appointed route after all.

I sat across from her. I pulled a handful of caramel corn out of a big cellophane bag. I offered her some under the distrustful eye of the mother. A game started between us. First, an unspoken effort to keep up the same rhythm as we crunched the sugary corn between our teeth, then swallowing and mimicking each other's expression of pleasure. Then she suddenly decided to change the game, and it became a true dialogue of clowning. Our cheeks ballooning as big as possible, we stuffed fistfuls of caramel corn into our mouths, then tried to swallow as much as we could without actually chewing it. The girl made a face like she was about to suffocate and clapped her hand over her mouth to hold back the explosive laugh she felt coming on. She was funny. I was grotesque. But I knew it. I was nearly euphoric. No one would doubt it if they had seen me. It amuses me, the awkward looks people throw my way when they're trying to avoid looking at me. Camouflaged behind newspapers, the other passengers took refuge in a hypocritical, irritated silence, broken by our laughter. The hilarity of a child is often infectious. But a monster who dares to have fun is bothersome: it keeps you from enjoying yourself and shrivels your own laughter into a grimace on the edge of your lips.

—

The mother had it in for me. Barely concealed disgust bloomed across her face. I had stolen what she thought to be her exclusive complicity with the girl. I am not displeased with myself.

—

She made the little girl get off the bus. I'm certain it was before their intended stop. The girl turned and waved at me from the sidewalk. Then the bus left. I didn't get up from seat when we got to the terminal. I made the trip again, in reverse. I opened another package of popcorn. Ten or so passengers took the place of the little girl; none of them dared look me in the face. I took some of the other routes that leave from St. Lazare. I traveled like this until the evening, pausing only to replenish my supply of caramel corn. I didn't laugh any more.

All the same, it was an agreeable day.

—

Latin Quarter. Rue de la Harpe. I am eating frenetically, finding my bliss in mountains of Tunisian pastry, drenched in honey and orange-blossom water. Macroutes[29], marzipan, corbeilles d'amour[30], znabias[31], cornes de gazelle. The mint tea hasn't quenched the thirst brought on by so much sugar. I'm gorging myself to death. My weight increases constantly. The difficulty I have fastening my skirts is proof. All the zippers are broken. Hooks and buttons pop off. Soon none of my dresses will fit.

—

Back to my room. My legs felt each stair on the way up. My fat-encrusted heart was pounding more wildly than usual. For the first time, seven flights of stairs seemed like an almost insurmountable challenge. I collapsed on the bed, my legs like cement.

Somnolence. When I awoke, I had the feeling of being trapped in an enormous block of ice that had been left in the desert to melt.

—

Warning signs. Unmistakable signs. Good signs.

—

Apologies to the mirror, but I already know I'm going to die hideous and deformed.

—

There is a Viennese pastry shop in the rue de l'École-de-Médicine that was somehow unknown to me. The Student introduced us. I'm short and the display window for the cakes is elevated, so I had passed it by a thousand times without ever noticing it. There are two or three steps at the front, and the entryway is very narrow. In a few weeks I may have trouble squeezing through. The day will come when I'll have to order my pastries from the street, unable to go inside. How soon will that be? How can I predict how quickly my flesh will expand?

The room is cozy, warm, intimate. Sitting side by side on the Naugahyde bench, we make an unusual couple in the mirror across the way. He doesn't notice. Or at least he pretends not to. Me, I'll forget nothing about this scene.

Close the eyes. Reconstruct the image. Give it a title: *La Bête et Le Beau*[32].

I take up at least two-thirds of the bench. Squashed into heaps of lumpy fat, I disappear. I'm practically at eye level with the table. The narrow chest of The Student overwhelms me with its slenderness. The cups and dishes are at mouth level. For a little while, the Beast even licks the plates to get at the residue of chocolate and cream that escaped from the spoons. My waxy skin presents a stark contrast to the robust health writ plain on the face of my neighbor. His cheekbones are high and rosy. Brighter traces, closer to red, marble his neck—a ruddy, sporting fellow, the collar of his shirt always slightly open. Mama would almost certainly call him "a handsome creature". That's the phrase she uses to describe young people she finds pleasing to look at. It's true that in the depths of his quartz-like eyes, there is a disturbing fixity that recalls the savagery of a wolf. But the comparison ends there. His warm, inviting, fluid voice betrays the acuity of his dark, overcast gaze. After closer examination, I find that he defies all of Mama's sociological classifications. He is too lavish with his smiles, too generously human to fall into any category of mere animal beauty.

His long, delicate hands—a little bony—remind me of the subtle elegance of a distinguished pianist, metamorphosing everything he touches, whether he means to or not. The ordinary dishes of the tea room become crystal and porcelain in his hands. The vulgar stainless steel utensils take on the weight and patina of old silver when he uses them.

Brushing away the heavy lock of dark hair that sometimes falls into his eyes, he has a particularly discreet gesture that I would describe as "princely". I'd guess he has the gift of a light touch, and the rare ability to give anything and feel everything with the same skimming caress.

My fingers are splayed out on the fake marble tabletop like shameless sausages, heavy and obscene. I pile them on top of each other, for lack of anywhere else to put them.

The Student's hand glides imperceptibly toward mine. His fingernails are glossy and they have no lunules. They progress, determined, toward imminent contact.

At the back of my mouth, my troubled saliva heads for more secret places. My hand brusquely snags its sugary prey from the nearest plate. I eat it in one mouthful.

The Beast strikes out at those who approach her. The Beast, in her beastly body, shelters neither a beautiful soul nor a Princess Charming. Besides, this Beast, locked in her sugared castle, has no other desire than to reveal all those fairy tales as lies. She turns away from the magic kiss that might deliver her from this form.

It may be that The Student can transform all that he touches. But he will not touch the Beast.

—

For three days now I have eaten nothing but honey. I'm experimenting with different varieties. I grade them, classify them, subject them to a process of elimination. Manuka honey[33] is the most exquisite. I douse my left forearm, hand to elbow. This takes up the entire jar because my arm is so thick, swollen like a child's balloon. Fortunately, I have smooth skin, with neither hair nor down. The honey spreads easily and sticks to my skin. It doesn't drip, like even the thicker jams do. And then I lick myself as diligently as any washing cat. I don't miss a single speck. My arm is tattooed with bluish-purple love bites. Then I go to bed. I roll over upon myself, at least as much as my bulk allows, and drool into my pillow. It's so pleasant to smell the trickle of sweet warmth flowing from inside of me.

Maybe this is what I could offer The Student: all that lost spittle. For free.

What else do I have to give?

—

My fat has mainly accumulated around my thighs and gut. Soon my stomach will protrude so far that I won't be able to see my sex. It will be hidden in a jewel-box of soft, curdled flesh: a paste gem, an imitation pearl, a nugget of fool's gold to be tossed aside in contempt.

This evening I put a mirror down on the floor to examine that red hole between my legs. It has never been of any use to anyone, and never will be, including me. Suddenly I was famished, with a violent cramping in my stomach. I drank some sweetened condensed milk straight from the container, sucking out the last few drops, my legs still spread over the mirror.

Fever and intense heat throughout my whole body. Electricity. A precise yet diffuse wave of energy circulating from my toes to my brain.

Manuka honey is heavy with the perfume of the great Australian oceans. A marvel discovered by some manufacturer of dietetic products. There is a manuka flower on the corner of the label, timid and velvety as an edelweiss in the hollow of a boulder. Smooth golden honey in a bulging little pot, which looks oddly like me.

—

Mama would carefully line up her small porcelain jars on the marble vanity, all of them childishly diminutive as a doll's tea set — the kind parents give to well-behaved little girls.She kept a whole range of cosmetics there — just the right hint of sweet almond oil, and creams infused with aromatic herbs in a range of dreamy colors. I often observed her make-up sessions, hidden behind a panel of draperies, my heart pounding. I had the delicious sensation of spying on a secret ceremony, some magic ritual for which I was too young to be an initiate. Mama's gestures fascinated me. Graceful and precise, in a fixed order, but in no way mechanical. A kind of ecstasy came over her. She was far away, very far away from me, from my father, from everything. It was clear that nothing else mattered but this lengthy communion with the mirror, and diligent concentric movements that smoothed the creams into her forehead, her cheeks, her neck. I admired her skill as a miniaturist. But then, I could barely hold a pair of tweezers without trembling. She measured out the exact infinitesimal quantity of eye shadow required to color each lid with incredible accuracy. She lacquered her nails with an expert hand, never needing to retouch them. She painted her lips an intense vermillion without a single smudge. She powdered her face moderately, with a sweep of the powder-puff that was almost a caress. Then she closed up all the little pots with her fingers held carefully apart to avoid chipping the still-fresh nail polish. A satisfied smile played across her lips as she brushed her hair. She tried different hairstyles, striking movie-star poses, then letting the tresses fall back down with an air of mock disapproval. After the extreme concentration required to apply her cosmetics, she could relax and dare to make her weird and impudent faces, naïve or shifty posturings that nobody would ever expect from her, except maybe my father. When she left the room, she would find her reserve and become once again the highly-visible wife of an equally high-powered diplomat. I think those interludes at the dressing table were a kind of meditation for her. An opalescent lampshade placed over the dressing table's light softened the glow. The rest of the room was in shadow, the velvet curtains not yet drawn. This, of course, permitted my own activities. Mama was awash in lamplight, as if she were in the spotlight at a theater. Her long negligee spread out around her, a ring of satin rose petals with glints of mother of pearl and coral. She was so far away. "Maybe she doesn't really exist," I thought. "Maybe she's just an apparition." Then she would rise with a gentle sigh and disappear into another room to dress. One time, she didn't come right back, so I took her place at the dressing table. The little porcelain jars were all in order, sparkling with an enticing brilliance, ready to be used in the next sacrament. There no longer any lights in the room, so I was operating in semi-darkness. I didn't want to see my own face suffused with the blushes either of pleasure or of the sensation of giving in to temptation. I used a counting rhyme that Zohra had taught me to pick out the one jar I would allow myself to open. I removed the lid with a trembling hand and tightly closed eyes. I guessed the color of the cream inside based on the scent. I knew them all. Only one was disagreeable to me. When chance brought me to the bizarre concoction of cucumber and avocado, I would cheat and start the game over to end up with a tiny sample of pale pink cream that smelled of irises. I spread it in a spiral on the back of my hand. And then my hand was no longer my hand, but a camellia petal, or Mama's hand—so soft, so transparent. I would have given all the candy in all the capitals of the world back then, in exchange for one little pot, redolent of iris, of honeysuckle, of freesia.

—

The creams smelled so good I could have eaten them. That was in Dakar. Or maybe London? I don't know any more.

It was somewhere in a dream. In solitude.

—

A distinct progression of my illness today.

An immense fatigue, ever since I woke up. Every time I move, my head spins. I haven't been to class in a week. I'm reluctant to go out, so I'm starting to dip into my emergency stash of supplies.

Uninterrupted sounds of chewing are my only music. Tireless labor of the stomach. Its capacity and endurance are sorely tested. Empty cookie packets accumulate around the bed and table. I force myself to move, to tidy up a little, to go outside. My palate is impatient. My tongue clamors for new sensations and fresh pastries. Going down the stairs isn't too hard. But later—a Calvary seven stories tall. What a stupid idea, deciding to live in a garret! Well, it's too late to move now.

—

Despite the fatigue, I drag myself down to the crêperie in rue Gregoire du Tour. I don't keep track of how many crêpes, dripping with butter and honey, go down my throat. It is an incomparable feast, paid for with a worrisome dizziness on the way back to the Métro. Now I have an idea of what awaits me from here on out.

A Sweet Death

—

The alarm has passed.

I thought the end had come. But no. It's easier to
move now. I feel as if I'm floating, more mentally than
physically. I dream of merging with the water. Is that the
reason my tastes are running to fruit juices? Milkshakes?
Ice-cream sodas and the polychromatic cocktails of the
Americans?

I'm done with the old tea-rooms and their fading charm
and their odors of hot ovens and caramelized apples. Now
I haunt the hamburger joints, drugstores, fast-food places.
I bathe in the neon and the musical hysteria.

My neck is swelling: a sponge saturated with lemonade
and strawberry-flavored milk. I fill myself to the brim.
I am overflowing. I spill over the cracked enamel of the
restrooms. I am decomposing.

—

I am infinitely pleased with myself.

—

Old Zohra was always part of the baggage we hauled
around from one country to the next. My mother said
she kept Zohra around because the old woman had no
rival when it came to laundering silk and satin lingerie.
All the others, the women of Martinique, the Hindus, the
Negresses, the Spanish, even the Frenchwomen ruined
her under-things, insolently disregarding the delicacy of
her lacy intimates.

Obviously, I had no say in any of this. But knowing Zohra was there in the kitchen, making clandestine offers of her fragrant neck — well, I for one was thrilled that we brought her along. Except for a few funny books, only Zohra in all the world could make me laugh when I was sad. She had an unshakeable fear of "the sorcerer bird" and always recited a thousand prayers before boarding a plane. Her enigmatic gestures to ward off the evil eye and deliver us safely to our destination would keep her busy for the remainder of the flight. Nothing could distract her from them.

The ritual recommenced with each trip. I once made up a lame excuse to have Zohra accompany me to the restroom. Once there, she offered up her neck, but her lips continued to murmur the incantations that would allow us to arrive in one piece. I shake with mad laughter just thinking about it. I am writing this with a freshly delivered frangiapane in front of me. I'm sure the other customers are all thinking — as my mother pointed out to me on that airplane — that I could stand to be a little more discreet. More discreet? With my size? And my blatant hideousness?

Zohra. Frangiapane. Her neck as flaky as thin pastry crust. Her kind, peaceful eyes, shaped exactly like sweet almonds. Ah, my old accomplice in those olfactory indiscretions.

———

At the Renoir[34] exhibit.

A Sweet Death

I wander through it this morning, nibbling at gingersnaps and coconut cookies as I go. Marks & Spencer have the best ones.

Long stops in front of feminine curves and fruity décors. My mouth distills the pleasure of crispness. My senses are on the alert: ears perked up, eyes searching the canvas, tongue staking a flake of coconut, fingers rustling in the open packet, nostrils identifying the high-end perfumes that permeate the air.

I proceed without difficulty among the visitors, a stumpy ambulatory cylinder, an unclassifiable silhouette, as long as their eyes are on the paintings. Otherwise the women scatter from my path, these ladies of the surrounding fashionable neighborhoods. They are women with nothing to do. They have run out of lovers, so they are regulars at the jewelers' and the tea-rooms, and yet they are the ones who never have any free time. One could probably locate my mother there in their midst. And why not? Anyway, my mother might appreciate the beauty of these nudes. She would still prefer Modigliani[35], with the streamlined bodies she so admires. She probably sees herself in them.

The women distance themselves from me almost instinctively, shocked, after their gracious surveillance of my most ungraceful curves. I am clearly an insult to their race. A compliment of the highest order!

I scoff at them through gnashing teeth. I drop cookie crumbs onto their lambskin boots. It is ersatz spitting—a childish pleasure, but a great one. The heat of the ginger inspires me to blasphemy. A woman seated on a bench, perhaps a blossoming forty, contemplates *La*

Danse à Bougival. A privileged moment, as it is still early, and the main crowd hasn't yet reached this far. She can enjoy the canvas on her own: innocent, ecstatic, lost in chromatic bliss, in the exquisite flight of the lines. But then I come along, brutally disintegrating her pleasure with an act of provocation that is becoming quite a habit for me. Planted right in front of the painting, I impose the vast bounty of my well-developed posterior right into her space, a posterior constructed upon massive rations of sugar, according to my own aesthetic conventions. The woman rises, bothered but still sympathetic. I can practically guess what she's thinking: "Well, we can't keep the infirm or the ill or even the monstrous from having access to art, too, now, can we?" I chuckle to myself.

Am I not also a masterpiece, in my own way?

—

Daily observation.

Before I start writing , I place an oval mirror flat on the table in the exact spot where I normally put my journal. I lean my head forward, tracking the signs of my metamorphosis. Not a single stage will escape me.

The flesh of my face lumps together, pulled down by its own weight. My cheeks fall in a soft mass, pigmented here and there with oily blackheads and tiny red veins. My eyes are lost among swollen, grayish-mauve folds. They no longer have their natural shape. There is no trace of a brow ridge now, let alone eyebrows. My eyelids are gummy furrows. Nothing is left but two moist brown slits in the surface of my skin, a fragile glistening, the memory of eyes. The contour of my chin has melted into the softness of a flushed, voluminous neck, where ganglia have floated to the surface but are impossible to locate with a finger. My heartbeat is audible, even amplified, like the echo of a toad's mucilaginous gullet.

My lips are floppy, greedy, fleshy appendages. They are the color of all the jams and jellies I have licked from them. They make a flaccid vent, voraciously gaping in an inarticulate cry for sugar.

Soon my cheeks will meet, resembling nothing so much as two ill-shapen buttocks. The still-intact cartilage of my nose will just barely poke out between them. I will be oblivious to that horrifying trough in the middle of my face. Anyone else would certainly attempt to hinder its progress with some elixir of youth. But my face will not submit to the chisel wielded by Time: no history will be inscribed here.

—

It seems as though, in those legends Zohra used to tell me, the scorpions weren't always that mean.

—

I watch myself grow fatter. I watch myself write, with my head just over the mirror and my cheek resting on the table. Seen in reverse, the nib of my pen is a tiny beetle trapped between my fingers. It is still active, lurching along on its curly, hooked feet, leaving a trail of shiny black slime. I like to watch it dry. It is an exotic yet still familiar witness to my continued existence as the peerless devourer, enveloped in her blanket of lard. The scribbling insect maintains an inventory of all the sugar I have tucked away—sometimes approximate, sometimes maniacally detailed, depending on my mood. It is a meteorologist of fortune, registering the daily turbulences of my gut: digestive stagnation or sheets of acid rain, the cloud cover of fatigue or the cyclones of insomnia.

It is by turns an undisciplined or docile little creature, reconstructing me into a past that refuses to accept me, a past I have not sought. Zohra's stories are the only parts I want to remember. It is a creature that follows its own mind, puking up ink as the nib moves along. Then it asks me why I write the things I do.

Why?

—

Mostly to prove that the person who claims to be me knew to step down from the summit of her own glorious sweetness, faithful to her promise to abandon the bitter farce that is this world. Just in time.

—

I just re-read the preceding. I swear, an excess of sugar made me write it. It's nothing but words. But weirdly lucid.

—

Well, Mr. Proust[36], I shamelessly eat my own madeleines[37] by the half-kilo. Sometimes my appreciation extends to an entire kilogram. I don't get them at the corner store, because—as I'm sure is clear by now—I have a highly refined taste for madeleines. Industrial manufacturing is repugnant to me, with its plastic wrapping, emulsifiers, preservatives and artificial flavorings. I am only satisfied by established quality: the little miracles performed in secret in real bakeries, using recipes that vary from one pastry chef to the next even if only by the merest hint of vanilla. Who could blame me for wanting to combine the necessary with the delightful? Pleasure with this slow preparation for my own death?

All the academic dissection of Proust's famous madeleine should probably have put me off eating them altogether. Just the other day, The Student was presenting one of his essays, rather pompously titled *The Rhetoric of Memory in Literary Creativity*. He was addressing the entire class, but his eyes kept moving back to me. In search of approbation? Or perhaps some other information? The silent apathy of our listless peers had to have been unbearable for him. They recorded every word, their pens racing across paper, not wanting to miss a single crumb of his work—all too content that someone else had been called to the blackboard. Only I paid attention, really looked at him, really listened to him, amused and skeptical like an old professor who has heard too many inept variations on "the short, plump cake" and all its evocatory capabilities.

Can I go on listening to The Student now that literature is no longer enjoyable? Now that I'm not sure why I even keep going to class? Now that madeleines stimulate nothing in me but my taste buds? Now that when they are dipped in tea, they are just a marvelous drug that manages to occupy my otherwise pointless existence?

Now that, instead of Proustian refinement, I prefer unspeakable gluttony? Now that lapses in my memory are filled in with ever-increasing quantities of sugar? How can I explain to him — without frightening him — that in the end, the dissolving power of death will confute both his intellectual exaltations and my own peculiar appetites?

He's still not finished with his analysis, comparisons, citations from the great authors, usage of academic verbiage, juggling of references. I force myself to look attentive. Frankly, I'm starting to get bored. And here he goes, back around to Proust. My thoughts take a few minutes of liberty, on a few brief flights of foolish fancy. For example: If I could only have one memory, which instant of my life would I choose? How many madeleines would I need to consume to make that memory click? How many times would I have to dip those madeleines into my tea for the illusory moment to be rebuilt in its entirety, with absolute exactitude? And so on, until the end of the presentation. I told The Student that I thought it was great. My sole purpose was to see him smile.

—

I am going to attempt a whole day of abstinence, so that I can try to remember one of Zohra's legends. But only one.

—

Well, so much for abstinence. Quite the contrary. I ate more hot waffles and more dried apricots than ever before. Then babas au rhum — a bit too spongy to be really good — then an amandine, and then a huge piece of chocolate studded with nuts.

A Sweet Death

So, I didn't actually practice abstinence, but the memory returned anyway, clear and colorful. Praise be to Monsieur Proust! I never would have expected so much.

From the time I started this journal—a few lines here, a few lines there, all the way up to the present when I am writing almost every day—that ink stain on the floor has been menacing me with its scorpion tail. I can't concentrate. I get up and grind it beneath my heel with my weight. It's the scrape of my shoe on the floor that finally makes the recollection fall into place.

The distant echo of an arthropodal shell cracking as it's crushed. Then louder, Zohra's relieved laugh at finding her yellowed teeth, their edges darkened with a greenish deposit. And then, closer still, her mirthful, delighted eyes in a maze of tiny wrinkles. Finally, her voice, triumphant: "Zohra always comes in time to chase away the scorpion!"

She and I were alone in the vast kitchen downstairs, all tiled in royal blue earthenware. Zohra braided my hair distractedly with one hand while humming one of the epic songs of her native land. It was a nostalgic time for her. Suddenly she leapt up, howling like a sorceress unleashed, and crushed the poor unfortunate creature, which she had just spied in the hollow of a loose tile. Her hatred assuaged and her laugh calmed, she sat down again, legs spread wide beneath a pile of multi-colored skirts. This pose meant she was about to tell a story. A true story for once. Not a legend. No, a story that had happened to me. Yes, to me, at an age when memory is still fast asleep in the mind, sunk in a slumber so profound that it needs someone like Zohra to waken it. There were lots of details, because she liked long descriptions as much as she enjoyed lengthy preambles leading up to the main event. She painted a picture of a wicker bassinet under the blue-tinted veil of the requisite mosquito netting. Inside it was the most beautiful baby in the world. Each part of my infant body inspired a welter of tenderness, which, honestly, made the story start to drag a bit. But she was so clearly enjoying herself that I couldn't bear to interrupt her—especially if that meant cutting short any of her praises of me.

I eventually learned how once, while I was innocently napping, a scorpion—goodness knows how it got in, but doubtless under the guidance of the evil eye—started to creep along the edge of the mosquito netting with undeniable criminal intent. The room was full of fresh air and light. My mother sat near me in her rocking chair, lost in her own mysterious reverie. Zohra was off elsewhere, dealing with all that delicate laundering she was paid to do.

"Then," she said, "a pin fell out of my hair, so I knew you were in danger. I ran, ran very fast to you. There were so many hallways and stairways in that house. I got water everywhere, all over the rug, my hands and feet were soaking wet. I kept running, then I saw Madame in her chair—Madame was staring at the scorpion but her eyes were not there, Madame wasn't moving, Madame was smiling at someone in her head. That scorpion, he was creeping down the net, right near your mouth. And Zohra arrived just in time to chase away the scorpion. And then Madame said, 'Zohra, get back to work.'"

The old woman nodded, then picked up a basket of beans and set to shelling them without another word. I carefully buried my nose in her neck for what felt like a very long time.

—

Ink spatter. An indelible stain in which I can now read a horrifying story. How I wish I had never heard it. I even tried washing the floor to get rid of it. My clumsiness only made it worse: diluted, the stain spread out even more.

—

For a while, everything was going fine. Or at least as usual. Crème de cassis went down my throat in little gulps of thick velvet. What a sweet new sensation. My tongue delighted in this utterly novel suavity, pure enchantment in my mouth. The level of liquid in the bottle went steadily down. I didn't really realize about the alcohol. Little by little, my eyes got bigger, globules of jade popping out of their sockets and turning in upon themselves. I was freed from my own heaviness, gone beyond time and space! I was a morsel of downy fluff waltzing with the light, an outrageous smile flashing in the night at the entire world.

I no longer existed. Tins of chestnut cream and canned fruit floated around me, an airborne carousel in my cramped room. I tried to catch the brass ring that would give me another turn on the ride. But all of a sudden the ride came screeching to a stop, braked by the collapse of a crumbling structure. A pile of jelly jars toppled over onto my foot and a flash of pain struck me up to the roots of my hair.

Once again I became a rock, a sponge drenched in molten lead, a viscous magma of clumpy lard. Yanked out of my usual rut by the alcohol, I betrayed my commitment to the weight, and now I am paying the price. I am overcome by a torpor so deep that I have decided to give up booze forever. Actually it's sort of a shame, since that crème de cassis really is delightful. Fighting a nearly irresistible urge to sleep. My pen traces nothing but thready symbols I probably won't be able to decipher later. Little scarab, drunk for once on liquor instead of ink, crashing into your own lines. You can't keep them straight. Marinating in your own juices, your own black vomit. You don't know what you're writing. You yawn, cross things out, color in the circles and loops of the letters. You pretend you're a crab. You amuse yourself with sloppy trifles — commas, circumflexes. You run words on top of one another without even noticing. You imprison your verbs in cages of bizarre scrawling. You spill your life story. You have nothing to say about anything except your own alcohol-fueled acrobatics. You certainly have nothing to be proud of, however much you try to pretend you do. You should put a hood over your shame, you drunken little pen, rabid scarab. Or tell me the story of your brother, the scorpion, who sleeps only a few dictionary pages away from you. But you can't feed me a happy story about the goodness in life, you shit-eating bug. You can't tell me to renounce the sugar, to renounce death. You are incapable of giving me a valid reason to keep going. Go to sleep. Keep your ghostwriting spittle to yourself until tomorrow. Quit your belching. You've watched my life so carefully. You've understood it, haven't you? So shut up and go to sleep, you useless pen.

A Sweet Death

Put your derisive words away, go to sleep. Death must
needs be lucid and

—

Yesterday's last word is lost in the oblivion of sleep. My
mouth feels pasty. Migraine. My eyes are so tired.

—

A long hard pull of grenadine syrup, the entire bottle
at one go. So pure. The straw plunges into a pool of
deliquescent rubies and blood comes rushing into my
mouth. Endless sucking. My lips trap the clear straw until
I have drunk the last drop of that divine liquid.

Milk without any sweetener added is horrifying to me. It
has the sour smell of gruel and fermentation. A musty,
stale, animal odor. The taste of raw flesh, of spongy
breasts.

—

My mother was never afraid of scorpions. She wanted to
be a beauty queen, not a mammal.

—

We go back to that Viennese bakery, that sinful den of
rapture for the connoisseur of the sugar-fueled orgy.
The Student asks me to order for both of us—whatever
I think would be the most mouthwatering. So we have
apple-cinnamon tarts, vanilla cheesecake and poppy-seed
brioches.

He forces himself to eat at my pace, very slowly, making
each bite melt away before swallowing it. He imitates

me in everything. When our plates are empty, he asks what we should have next. He hurries to order from the astonished waitress, who is obviously unused to such ferocious appetites. Without comment, and almost naturally, he spends the next two hours copying my gestures, my gustatory curiosity, my pleasure and my greed, my interminable swallowing, all of my quirks. He isn't mimicking me in a cruel way. No, he is showing me an accurate reflection of myself. I am not taken in by his game.

He has thrown out an unspoken wager. So be it. All the pastries in this shop couldn't have made me refuse it. Because nobody can beat me at my own game. But him? He isn't used to the rich creams, the heavy chocolates. How far will he really be able to take this?

I don't take my eyes off him. Smiling, so nonchalant, he is on the verge of passing out but doesn't let it show. He keeps up the struggle with the reserved passion of a chess player, doggedly trying to unravel the secret strategies of his adversary.

Then I imagine him back in his room at the dormitory. I see him, eyes yellow and sick, arms clutching his stomach, spasms shaking his body. His toilet overflowing with reeking puke. A little note pinned to his door, forbidding any disturbance until further notice. I hear him cursing himself for this ridiculous wager and its consequences. My complacency and derision rip cries of anger from his lips. He ponders the futile absurdity of his attempt to draw me back into the world of graceful femininity. Between waves of nausea, he still feels a sense of pride—philanthropy, even. Refusing defeat, he vows to rescue me. He knows

he can pull me back from the brink of despair. He is
sure he can restore my interest in life, give me a taste for
men. He will become my faithful swain, my hero, the
luminous center of my universe, the axis around which
my existence will revolve. But, while he is waiting for this
to happen, pain is boring into his head and his gut. In my
eyes, he becomes so frightful in his grimacing that I cry
Uncle out of concern for his beauty.

"What are you trying to prove here?" I ask him. "I don't
need a mirror. I look at myself quite enough. In fact, it's
pretty much all I do. I know who I am, what I look like,
and the effects I produce. It's all intentional. Deliberate
and consented to."

These words spring out of me, brutal, with a deep and
unexpected violence. With one fell stroke I break our
tacit—and prudent—agreement to avoid mention of
our personal lives. Usually nothing of our inner worlds
comes out during our long discussions. But by performing
his imitation, wasn't he the first to force his way into my
territory? As I made my carefully detailed plan for a slow
death, I had foreseen everything but the unforeseeable:
the intrusion of a stranger who is not only interested in
my behavior, but who seeks to turn me from it.

"You don't really mean that, do you? About who you are?
There is so much suffering inside you that you've never
let out. Ever since I met you I've been trying to find out
why."

Such a nonsensical preoccupation! It sparked my sense
of hilarity and laughed until I almost choked: a wild,
resonant laugh.

"You should write dialogue for the movies," I say, after I catch my breath. "There's no point going through all the bad stuff. Keep your answers. Use them someplace else, where they might actually do some good. And stop eating. You'll never be able to digest all that cake."

He takes my advice, at least as far as the cake is concerned. But his cheeks are suffused with blood, with suppressed anger. His emotions are written clearly on his face. It's almost touching.

Then we leave the pastry shop as if nothing has happened.

—

When will he stop with the pointless questions? What he's trying so hard to understand is really very simple. All I have to live for is sugar.

—

Midterms are coming up. I continue imperturbably upon my sugar path with a free spirit. I'm in the bakeries more than the library. So what? I'm surrounded by anxiety, panic, feverish study, note-taking, last-minute cramming, close-bitten nails, dark-circled eyes, fear, or a false nonchalance about the approaching tests. Students always find the exam subjects so distressingly trite. "These topics—so banal!" they say. But they always use the same tired clichés in their own oh-so-revolutionary responses. Well, I should give Mama her due for making the task easier for me. I was stuffed full of books and introduced to the finer points of literary analysis at a very early age. I acquired a cultural education and developed critical

faculties that far outstrip any of my classmates. Not that
I'm trying to blow my own horn or anything.

No need to study. I'm only working on sugar. No
more reading. I never did anything but read—and
passionately, at that—back when I refused to eat sweets.
Mama showered me with both books and chocolates,
not realizing that I couldn't ingest both at the same
time. A season for each fruit. An age for each form of…
nourishment.

So, no more books now. The words of others stick too
close in my memory, too close to my pen. To the point
where I sometimes have to wonder if I am in fact the
author of what I write here.

No more books. They have given way to sugary food and
culinary critiques.

No more books. I have swallowed them all, for whole
nights and entire days, in all climates, at the four
corners of solitude and boredom. Books were my only
companions—with their knowing murmurs and mocking
laughs echoing from the bookshelves—on those evenings
when we were hosting receptions. I could hear the music,
too: tangos or waltzes. Books, my voiceless universe
of countless lives and countless deaths, my hatred, my
apocalypses, my resurrections, my metamorphoses, my
invented ages, my playground, my schoolgirl pranks,
played without the school. Books were a teeming,
ferocious jungle in the middle of the geometric splendor
of the embassy gardens. Books were my theatre of mirth,
where Mama flew off the stage in a rustle of whirling silk.
Books were my refuge, my little square of sky just visible
from a gilded prison cell. Books were the barometer

and mirror of my state of mind. There were books with
their pages ripped out, never offering any rebuke. Books
deciphered by moonlight on deserted balconies. Books
galore, enough to make my memory and my eyes burst.
Books were a solitary pleasure, never shared. Some of
the books I still look at, even now. It kind of makes me
want to vomit. I knew just enough to shut down the first
know-it-all to cross my path. Childish vanity! That flashy
arrogance still keeps me bound to the inherent stupidity
of our species. But oh, not for much longer! Soon, all my
glory will be in my weight.

In a few weeks, after the literature examinations — which
I will finish brilliantly and in record time — I am going
to indulge in an ice-cream sandwich in one of my old
neighborhood cinemas. It's the kind where the red curtain
still rises solemnly to reveal the screen. Meanwhile, all the
slender people, the svelte, the nervous, the bony, will still
be sweating over those banal exam topics.

—

I'm in great shape. This isn't normal.

—

Those pastry chefs are geniuses. True artists, whose work
I have discovered completely on my own. Not like all
those writers.

—

Springtime. Bare arms, uncovered shoulders. I know,
because I read it somewhere, that the sap is on the verge
of boiling. The flame of desire rises in men's eyes. Girls
feel their still-translucent cheeks flush with pleasure.

A Sweet Death

According to the literature, since the dawn of time springtime has been this and only this: unceasing chatter about the various ways in which people's love lives give them grief. Do they have to go on about it so? Why do they get so worked up about it just because the skies are clear and the sun is out? Exhibiting all that skin, forgetting that the skin is just a husk holding in a soggy, sticky mass? Congregating in a mess of erotic magma?

I'm happy just to sweeten my blood with cherries. I cram myself full of them. Oh, for springtime to weigh me down with strawberries and plump, white-hearted cherries. My mouth will overflow with pits kept too long beneath my tongue. The café terraces will fill with smiling people seeking one another out. What would it take for them to believe in paradise? If I had a pea-shooter, I would sink the lemon twists in their aperitif glasses with the cherry stones of contempt.

A different spring day, like this one but more intense; a tunnel of bougainvillea bristling with the buzz of insects. The embassy gardens were deserted. It was siesta time. Mama was balanced gently on her chaise-longue, eyes half-closed, arms spread out, legs slightly parted beneath her straw-yellow organdy robe. Crouched behind a privet hedge, I watched her from between the interlaced leaves. An enormous boil was eating away at the middle of my chin. Afraid of being noticed, I withstood the burning itch without flinching. Suddenly—a figure beneath the arch of bougainvillea, just behind Mama. A man in a light suit. The Spaniard. I recognized him immediately, even though I'd only seen him once before. A memorable event. I was very young then. I had escaped Zohra's

usually watchful eyes. She was supposed to have put
me to bed, but I burst into the salon where the guests
were mingling before dinner. My cheek still burns
with all the pinches he inflicted upon it. He called me
"pequeñita mia" several times in his gravelly voice, a
bit authoritarian, a bit harsh, in spite of the pleasure he
seemed to derive from calling me by that name. He put
down his glass and picked me up in his arms, lifting me
over his head like a trophy. He burst into laughter, all
of his teeth showing, looking at my mother the entire
time. But Mama didn't laugh. She slowly tucked a lock
of hair behind her ear, apparently to calm some anguish
that caused both her and the half-smoked cigarette in
her hand to tremble. The Spaniard kept his proprietary
grip upon me. His eyes shone with alcohol and pride. He
began to spin around and around, clicking his heels in
a flamenco beat. I thought he might never put me back
down, that we would stay like this forever, caught between
heaven and earth, the focal point and laughingstock of
the adults who were applauding him, won over by his
euphoria. Mama suddenly cried, "Enough!" and it all
ended—the laughing, the dizziness, the terror. She took
me in her arms, my head pressed to her bosom: time to
go back to my room. Her heartbeat was a wild tempest of
thudding. The pin of her brooch scratched my chin. She
stormed up the stairs in something akin to rage. I could
hear the nervous clinking of her silver bracelets.

The next day Zohra was fired, and access to the salon
was strictly forbidden to me, at least during receptions. It
was at this point, I think, that the little parcels of candy
first started to appear on my nightstand. The first ones
were lovely: fat, shiny dates stuffed with bright-pink and

pistachio-green marzipan. To this very day, though, I've never actually tasted one.

How long have I been at this table? Writing has exhausted me. The sun is starting to beat down, even here under the roof of the attic. The flock of pigeons on the windowsill emits a fetid stink. Thick grenadine syrup is my beverage today. Liquid rubies, too sweet to adulterate or dilute, especially since I don't have any ice cubes to chill water. I've bought some stuffed dates. An insane craving for them gave me the strength to go out. These dates are a marvel. Their lethal weight is expanding in my gut.

———

I must have perspired a great deal. The notebook paper is curled and wrinkling, damp under the pressure of my hand, which has been moving across the page in fits and starts. I pass my tongue between my burning, sweaty fingers. The taste of salt surprises me. I had forgotten it. I guess I believed that I now exuded a sugary liqueur, but no. Apparently nothing has gone that far awry with my bodily functions. My sweat has the same unbearably normal taste as anyone else's. The ink is infused with salt as soon as it touches the damp paper. My handwriting seems moth-eaten, spongy, an artifact created by a drunkard.

———

The boil exploded. I wiped up the pus that ran down my neck with a leaf plucked from the privet hedge. In my chest, my heart exploded as well. Because of my mother, because of The Spaniard, because of some great violence that had been done. I ran away, far away, so I wouldn't have to see what happened next underneath that canopy of flowers.

Even today, it is a gaping hole in my memory. The Muslim cemetery extended down to the sea. Children made a huge ruckus as they played among the tombs. One of them offered me a fistful of pistachios. Sunset found me asleep, face-down in the sand.

—

I think that was the day I decided to make myself ugly.

—

Zohra fired! Was her sin so great that she deserved such wrath from my mother? What grave calamity had she unleashed by letting me go into the reception hall? Children pull these unexpected tricks all the time. They are often surprised and agitated by strangers. And The Spaniard was very impressive. My cries, when he lifted me up in his arms, were they really so shocking? And anyway, I had made everyone laugh, all of the important gentlemen and lovely powdered ladies who had come to drink and dance on the Embassy's dime.

Fortunately, Mama couldn't find a laundress as skilled with silks as Zohra was. She called Zohra back into her service shortly afterwards. Zohra didn't hesitate. She swallowed her pride, her dignity—the injured servant, victim of an injustice, subjected to the whims of her mistress. She came back.

"For you," she whispered in my ear.

—

I've written so much the last few days. I don't really
talk much anymore. I don't really even pay attention to
speech, either. Nothing is allowed to enter my memory.
I no longer write in accordance with the random dictates
of time or content. I no longer hear anything but the
machinery of my own digesting body. Respiratory hissing.
Sucking noises. Swallowing. Gastric churning. Hiccups.
Belches. Intestinal disturbances.

—

Pommes d'api[38], lacquered red and delicious. The joy of
oily doughnuts rolled in sugar. Barbe à papa[39], which suits
this monster so well. There is a carnival on place Pigalle.
Carnivals aren't really my thing—everyone here has a
touch of the grotesque, so I go pretty much unnoticed.

I wish I had the pleasure of feeling out of place, but
instead it's just the pleasure of sugar here.

—

The square at Tour Saint-Jacques[40]. Wee hours of
the morning. Like a yogi saluting the sun, I have just
completed the lengthy ritual of force-feeding myself.
After an endless night of insomnia and no provisions to
save me, a breathless night in that humid airless garret,
I am here on a bench at the only hour the hordes of city
folk are still asleep. The only time I can promenade my
bulk through the streets without the flesh of strangers
pressing up against my own. It is the hour of contented
misanthropy. I relish this moment in a city that seems like
an immense cake in which I have no share—

—

Stretched out on a bench, legs bent, notebook propped up on thighs. I find that I don't actually feel all that well. Maybe the dozen hot butter croissants I just devoured are weighing down my stomach. There are few things harder to digest than a pastry straight out of the oven, still impregnated with a yeasty savor. How can one resist? Drawn by the fragrance of baking bread, seized by salivary impatience, I flung myself desperately into the oven-room of an already-open bakery where the morning boy had just brought out the first piping-hot batch of bread and croissants.

Now vertigo and a sour feeling in the pit of my stomach. I don't know if it's me or the Tour Saint-Jacques that's swaying, but at risk of upsetting the surrealists out there, there's nothing all that sunflowery about that particular building. Not even to my skewed vision, eyelids closing bit by bit, until the only lights they admit are the tiniest slivers of phosphorescence.

—

I awoke to a tap on my shoulder. A suspicious policeman, imagining me to be a drug fiend, a whore, a bum, or maybe just an amnesiac. I declined to give my identity, explain my presence or show my papers. On the last page of this notebook, I jotted down a few words by André Breton[11] in front of the cop:

"*In Paris, the wobbling Tour Saint-Jacques*

Is just like a sunflower."

Ring by ring, I tore the paper from its spiraled metal binding. As if it were an epistle of the utmost importance, I handed it to him with a solemn gesture. Yes sir, this pile of sagging flesh upon the bench, this caricature of a woman—or so you obviously think—who composes verses at daybreak, this false poet, is in fact the daughter of a high-ranking diplomat. You can check it in your files. But that still won't tell you everything. It won't tell you about my unshakeable determination; my amusement at your air of having stepped onto some far-off alien planet. Oh, how I shall exult, from the other side, on the day you break down my door to find the massive purplish bag of skin that envelops my corpse: faithful to sugar right to the bitter end.

—

I have few accomplices. Only an old lady I met at La Gourmandise understood me. She even made a few recommendations to me. Irremediably thin, she was nevertheless a true sugar fiend. Thanks to her, I made the acquaintance of the house extravaganza, "The Platter of Hercules" at a nearby Greek restaurant. It is a dessert that definitely lives up to its name. Four columns of twisted meringue, supporting a cloud of Chantilly cream above an ocean of liqueurs that was drowning a rainbow of sorbets. Cries of admiration invariably greet this creation as it is brought to a table. The maître d'hôtel, flattered but discreet, flashes a restrained smile and withdraws. The silence of a cathedral hangs over the room. No, the silence of enjoyment preoccupied with itself. Most people never finish this titanic dessert. Apparently I am the only one ever to order it twice.

—

The downpour catches me in front of a bookstore. I use the opportunity to consult the photography section. I finally discover the work of Diane Arbus. Such pretty little monsters. Such lovely pictures she has made of them — placing the scandal of their unfortunately distributed flesh at an even greater distance from the world. Extraordinary photos, to be sure. But their adulatory beauty negates the monstrosity. Anesthetized monsters, odorless, without texture. How will the world understand the burden of a megalomaniacal stomach, the too-soft feel of deliquescent rolls of fat, the shocking insolence of the loudly burbling gut? Who will tell of the complacency of the monster who knows she is a monster — if not that monster herself?

I will tell that story.

The monsters in this book keep quiet. I see nothing of myself in them.

—

Returning to one's own species is all the more painful when one has been actively trying to escape that species. Here I am, back at the level of mollusks, which I have struggled to transcend by venturing along the higher paths of intellect. To raise myself to the level of vertebrates, I manufactured a carcass for myself, plus a skeleton to hold it up. Granted, I didn't exactly make any haste in getting it to grow. My neck held upright, my gaze climbed the silhouettes of adults for a long, long time. Their faces lost in the heavens, gleaming under iridescent fires that I mistook for suns. Mama's smile was ensconced at a dizzying height, coagulated in a pool of impeccable red. Her eyes, ringed in ebony, glittered like inaccessible stars that had somehow settled into the eye-sockets of a statue on a pedestal. I knew almost nothing of my father—a big blond fellow with that Viking coldness—except his huge strong legs and their supple movement beneath the cream-colored fabric of his summer trousers. Chocolate meteorites fell with clockwork regularity upon this low-angle world, populated with marble giants. Rocky concretions encrusted with almonds or hazelnuts, or sometimes streamlined barley-sugar missiles in shells of yellow cellophane. Produced in the far-off reaches of a forbidden galaxy, these sweets frightened me a little. Even so, up on my tiptoes, I would reach up a hand to those entities who dispensed all that sugary manna. But their gazes were always elsewhere, aligned with the implacable horizontal plane inhabited by other beings their size.

I quit growing any taller. Without realizing it, I was back on track to my own race. But one does not renounce one's species with impunity. Today my bones are dissolving in the formaldehyde of intractable fatigue. My spine sags under the onerous burden I have loaded upon it. Vanquished by the weight, I will simply crawl along. A weak, flaccid blob; I won't even have the dignity of the manatee, who can at least throw her head up out of the sea to cry out to her own kind.

———

How long has it been since my arms could go all the way around my body?

—

Mama set a date to meet me in Brussels on her way back to Madagascar. She didn't say anything about why she'd been back in Europe.

I didn't reply. I have the excuse of the exams. Seeing her again would produce no emotional response, no surprise. I'm well aware of her consummate artistry in the realm of self-representation. She'll paint her cheeks with that bright flush of color that simulates travel fatigue. I can guess to what degree she will try to appear natural. Jet lag, the shock of a different climate, night after night of long parties and soirées—none of these leave a mark on her. The firm flesh of her face has yet to show a single wrinkle. And I can tell you right now, we would speak of nothing of the remotest importance. The paintings of the Dutch Masters would take the place of actual conversational topics. Maybe Baudelaire's views on Belgium. Such inconsequential exchanges just wouldn't be worth the trip.

—

Anyway, I promised myself that I wouldn't reveal myself to her until their final return from Madagascar.

—

And yet, I'm quite sure I'll eventually submit to her summons. She's stronger than I am.

I'm going to Brussels.

—

Another restless night, at least mentally. I'm living in an effervescent state of anticipation over my departure, which has been scheduled for tomorrow morning. It's not so much the idea of seeing her again that's keeping me awake. No, it's the prospect of three hours on the train with nothing to do but gorge myself on sweets. What a thrill! My travel bag contains more candy than clothing. It's a struggle not to start in on them right now. It's so very tempting to just dig into the stash and open up a packet of Cadbury Fingers[42]. But I know that if I start, I won't be able to stop, and then I'll have to pack all over again. And I already spent half the day carefully selecting those items I thought would please me the most on this trip.

I keep busy with trivial things to help resist that temptation. Tracking down crumbs of chocolate in the folds of crumpled aluminum wrappers. Recovering the crispy dust from a partitioned cookie box. Measuring the exact level of my syrup stores, set above the glasses ranged on the windowsill. Scraping the solidified drippings from the edges of the honey jars. Carefully fingering through the wool of the carpet to extract a crumbling raisin. Searching in my pockets to see if one single savior of a bonbon has escaped my nibbling. Then under the bed, on the bed, in the bed—I overturn the wastebasket, the bread box, my leather schoolbag. Desperate, I turn to counting the rolls of fat on my thighs and arms.

Insomnia drags me back to thoughts of the present. What is The Student doing at this hour of the night? I didn't tell him I was leaving. Will my absence worry him? Because I certainly intend to take my time in Brussels, exhausting all the charms of the Belgian pastry shops before returning to Paris.

The Student. A mere slip of a man who would melt like a bonbon between my thighs. A naïve, careless Jonah, flinging himself to the aid of the whale. He and Mama are rare specimens yanked upward from the rest of the potbellied, simian specimens of the human race. Tomorrow I will pay tribute to the ugliness in this world. But I doubt anyone will shower my efforts with any praise.

—

On the train. My pen jolts with the lurching of the car. So much for the silky glide of ink upon smooth paper. The page is covered with raspy scratches. It's like finding a crumb of yeast from a poorly-baked chausson aux pommes[43] stuck in your tooth. I should probably just stop trying to write. And there are still plenty of cookies.

—

Still on the train, just back from the toilet. An unbearable nausea has put me off track. I can't eat another thing. Heave upon heave of vomit. My repeated trips to the end of the car intrigued the other first-class passengers. I staggered along the rhythm of the train making me feel drunk. Despite the width of the aisle, I just barely avoided falling flat onto an elderly gentleman, absorbed in his newspaper. I saw the familiar look of disgust and pity in his eyes. I had no time to apologize nausea doesn't wait. Train toilets are not made for people my size. I felt like I was being compressed.

Brussels isn't too far away now. The absolute last thing I need is to appear ill in front of Mama.

—

The hotel is very…ordinary. I am frankly astounded that Mama got me such a modest, commonplace little room. Then again, I'm even more astounded that she wanted to see me at all.

—

She came in without knocking. Her hand flew to her mouth, suppressing a cry of revulsion. I didn't expect so much from her. She was wearing a perfectly ravishing pair of white lace gloves.

The cramped room forced us into a physical proximity we hadn't shared in a very long time, one which we had both nearly forgotten. She was in the lizard-skin armchair. I was barely seated, perched on the edge of the bed. My grossly swollen foot brushed against the varnished needle of her stiletto heel. Her breath was almost palpable, a potent mingling of raspberries and tobacco. Her voice occupied the space between us, warm and flowing as she praised the ambience of Brussels, betraying a hint of bitterness at any mention of Madagascar.

She spoke at length about the suffocating heat of the island, about how her nerves were frayed by the unbearable noise of the birds and the insects, the never-changing scenario of all diplomatic missions, the maddening inefficiency of the native staff at the consulate.

"Thank heavens I have Zohra."

And about Zohra, not a single word more. She wouldn't have said anything about Father, either, if I hadn't asked for news of him. The question visibly upset her. The hint of a furrow between her eyebrows, the quiver of her lip beneath its flaming red paint, and then the smile that returned almost immediately, immobile and impeccable.

She talked for a long time, but the charm was short-lived. She knew how to express her passion for literature and art, but she was less able to discuss her travels probably because she had virtually no interest in any of the countries to which she had followed my father. Little sighs of resignation, of nostalgia for Paris escaped her breast from time to time. She envied me for not being subjected to the florid debauchery of tropical climes, the violent contrasts, the complete absence of moderation and subtlety and refinement.

She set to lecturing me about the great Flemish painters with the same seriousness I recalled from our literature lessons. Again I had the feeling that she was counting out the time precisely, and that our interview would not exceed the standard two hours.

I couldn't have cared less about the jubilant little world of frozen canals, or the phantasmagoria of Jérôme Bosch[44], or the icy innocence of the painted Virgins with which she tried to embellish the empty space of the cheerless hotel room. So much for her verbal magic. I had stopped wondering why she was in Brussels, or what this visit was supposed to mean. The tips of her fingers fascinated me more than the *Icarus* of Brueghel the Elder[45]. Agile dancers, moving freely in traceries of lace, they tapped the scarred arm of the chair. A flight of delicately embroidered gloves, crocheted caresses of Scottish thread, secret blossoms. And, striking a chord with the hands of my mother, I saw the hands of The Student.

—

I saw her, veiled properly all in black, before an immense hole that had been excavated for a coffin of remarkable proportions. A graying man, with an austere but attentive face and the air of a distinguished professor, or maybe a barrister, affectionately gave her his arm. Behind them, shriveled and twisted, hands covering her face, Zohra sobbed, lurched, her feet imprisoned by an inextricable jumble of skirts.

In the background, The Student was seated on a block of granite. Trying to remain unnoticed. His breath caught at the woman's inhuman, undeserved beauty. She stooped in a slow wave of fabric to take up a fistful of earth in her ungloved hand. It was an unknown substance to her—ever impassive, she didn't let the unpleasantness of the sensation show. On the contrary, she was very dignified as she powdered the still-fresh lacquer of the casket with dirt from her fingertips.

Slowly, she unbent her body, as if she had all of eternity. As she rose, her eyes met the gaze of the fascinated young man. In that silent, furtive exchange, he thought he could detect the satisfaction of flattered vanity, the subtle signal of invitation, the shadow of an acquiescent smile. He stayed there, bewildered, between rapture and dread, dumbly setting himself to the task of counting the clods of soil beneath which my sugary laugh had at last managed to disappear forever.

—

The allotted time is already up. My mother has slipped on a jacket of raw silk, reassembled her parcels, uttered a few noncommittal words of advice, placed a vermillion kiss upon each of my cheeks, and closed the door to the hotel room behind her.

In her place on the armchair is a beribboned box, which I do not open.

—

I wrote those last few lines just after Mama left, and they exhausted me. With her, time is never elastic. I wanted it to stretch out between each word as a reassurance that she really been there a few minutes ago, seated in the armchair in front of me. The two hours had flown by, sugar all but forgotten. If the housekeeper hadn't knocked this morning, I would probably still be sunk in a slumber almost as heavy as me.

At this very moment my mother is defying the laws of gravity and flying off, back to Madagascar. Or wherever.

I board the plane too—a terrorist with no other weapon but my massive bulk, menacing the other passengers with my excessive weight. The other travelers eye me suspiciously, except for the very lovely, very chic woman who smiles out the porthole at the man who accompanied her to the gangway. She blows him a kiss from her fingertips, which are gloved in white lace.

No one raises an alarm. Too bad for them, because after the plane takes flight, I will explode in a starburst of candied flesh.

—

Writing empties me of all substance. It's time to explore the pastry shops of Brussels. The gift box is still sitting

there. That's fine—I don't need the armchair. It's much
too narrow to fit me.

—

Ah, Belgium! Happy land of sugary abundance!
Disparaged so unjustly by Baudelaire! But then, he
consumed little besides hashish and opium…

In Brussels, indolence parades itself about in open
carriages. It sets rendez-vous in teahouses draped in
magnificently heavy tapestries. Glowing red windows are
impeccably arranged. The world is a frozen lacy maze
in which an entire society of elderly ladies spreads out
generous bones without compunction. They abandon
themselves to the delights of pastry. An accomplice in
their joyful lust, I am the lucid one. I am the same age
as their wrinkles and their gassy stomachs. But they are
undertaking this journey into sugar's domain so very late
in life. I'm champing at the bit, sparing myself the long
slow bother of the years, avoiding the trick of seduction at
the age of twenty, side-stepping the mirage of love and the
bitterness of crumbling dreams. The fundamental inanity
of existence has already pierced my heart, and I know
now that only cakes have any savor.

I find them sympathetic, these little old ladies. They burst
into laughter as they gobble down their chocolate and
raspberry mousses. All cares about waistlines or corsets or
girdles have been discarded. Their noses in their custards,
they recall their compressed stomachs, their imperfect
figures, the cunningly insidious cellulite that must be
massaged away with a horse-hair glove. No more tortures
now, ever. They surrender, wide-mouthed and big-

bellied, delivered from their frustrations, satisfied by the weight of their own substance, happy at last to spend the afternoon in sweetened communion over a cup of coffee.

I follow them everywhere. Perhaps my fate will be fulfilled in the comfortable warmth of their meeting places. I enter their ghetto—physically fat and mentally ready for any excess. I want sugar right now—now and forever—with any and all of its attendant consequences.

—

So, it's a portable bathroom scale. One of the ones that you tuck in between the tub and the bidet, hidden away so that nobody suspects how much care you actually take to keep in shape.

My mother bought it at a nearby pharmacy. I'll bet they were surprised when she asked to have it gift-wrapped.

What touching attention to detail. A bulls-eye, wrapped in gold. But for once my mother has missed the mark. The needle is irretrievably stuck at the maximum weight, fixed at one hundred kilos. This tells me absolutely nothing about my actual weight.

—

Oh, the sadness of a hotel room at this late hour, when all the pastry shops have closed and I have nothing but this rickety scrap of a table to write on, under the grainy, wavering light of a neon sign.

A presentiment: we will not see each other again. Her little handkerchief was scented with freesia, a perfume that suits her so beautifully.

A Sweet Death

—

A lovely morning. The sun filters in through the dusty
veil of the drapes, giving the room a slightly more
engaging look. I've put the scale on the edge of the table:
my breasts come exactly to its level. Blouse unbuttoned,
chest bared, I hoist them vigorously, imitating the
straightforward tussling in those Flemish paintings of
wedding-night scenarios. My nipples have the supple,
compact consistency of those rubbery dolls whose arms
and legs can be twisted and contorted however you wish.
The only difference between my breasts and the dolls is
that my breasts don't pivot on their axes quite so far. And
they don't squeak when I press on them. I lift them to my
nose and sniff them. I examine their smooth transparency,
the stretched skin, well-scrubbed and piglet-pink, veined
with blue and stained with light patches of red. I will
weigh them presently. The sun is warming the platform of
the scale, so I will be spared the discomfort of cold metal.

—

Heavy with accumulated fat, my natural protuberances
spread out all over the place. The indicator gauge, no
doubt skewed by my earlier successive attempts to weigh
my entire self, disappears under the pillow of my splayed
breasts.

So I still don't know the weight even of that which
precedes me.

—

This country is a permanent incitement to the ingestion
of sugar: the simplest cup of coffee or tea is served

with a cookie or a chocolate. Or both. Sometimes there's a choice of sugar varieties to sweeten your drink: granulated, brown, or cubes. So many small considerations, not easily dismissed or forgotten. Baudelaire was such an ingrate.

—

My dissolution gladdens me. I visited a dozen pastry shops today. Such fatigue. Immense fatigue. But absolutely no desire to return to Paris.

—

On the Grand-Place in Brussels.

The tourists let themselves be photographed by a zealous young man who knows how to approach them with an audacity and seductiveness that convinces them that they should let him do it. They pose, playful or downright clownish. They shake the Polaroid frantically, impatient for the results, then blow on it to make the image appear faster. Then, having found themselves, they laugh and go away arm in arm, noses in the air, ecstatic, lost in Baroque luxury, illuminated by the sumptuous glow of the sun, whose light now inundates the plaza. The photographer is making such an effort that only a few people pass up the chance for Polaroid immortality. His pockets fill as he sells off these instant souvenir banalities that will fatten up the travelers' vacation albums.

From the café terrace where I have just consumed an edifice of ice cream as Baroque in construction as the architecture that surrounds me, I watch his games, and

those of the tourists. The main thing for him is payment.
He produces his photos without concern for his subject.
But his customers covet only the contents of that moist
rectangle of freshly-captured memory, which he holds out
to them at the end of his fingertips, like a used tissue.

What traces will I leave? What will be my posthumous
legacy in the memory of mankind?

A fat girl met upon the sidewalk, to whom one ceded the
right of way simply because she took up more space. A
dwarf encased in lard who sat and wrote on the terrace
of the same café where one went for drinks. A little chunk
of a woman, repellently ugly, who thrust her hand again
and again into a bag of cookies on the platform at the
Gare Saint-Michel. A slovenly undesirable in the middle
of a cute little tea-room. One of the dregs of humanity in
an elevator in the XVIe arrondissement[16]. A freak-show
monster traveling in a first-class train car. Strong images.
Disagreeable images. Gripping images for those who seek
them. For others—no sooner seen than blocked out.

Will the photographer accost me too? He would have to
frame the shot from rather far away in order to get all of
me into the viewfinder. And all I have to do is cross the
plaza to find out.

———

Back to my notebook.

He did not propose his services to me. I had to solicit
them. He trembled with embarrassment. The picture was
out of focus, I pointed out. In any case, the result matters

little to me, I added, when I suggested that we try again. It is the provocation that interests me. And the proof that I seem to affect people more than I really should be able to.

The photographer has just left the plaza.

—

A sunny afternoon. Life seems good to me for a little while. An hour of nonchalance against a backdrop of polished woodwork. A little portentous, perhaps, but aerated by an abundance of green plants that practically breathe health. I am well, here on this Naugahyde bench, upon which my buttocks are discreetly perspiring. The room is bathed in the hot, close odors of yeast, liqueurs, brioches. The pastry chef here has some real talent. The mokas, the bavaroises[47], the charlottes[48], all have the same unblemished glaze as the Flemish skies depicted by the Old Masters. I have already paid my respects to the succulent fraisier[49]. And now a freshly deposited bourbon mousse sits before me on a silver plate, which makes it all the more appetizing. I eat slowly, little spoonfuls between sentences. A canary is in a cage suspended from the ceiling, gluttonous as I am. He neglects his morsel of cuttlefish bone to sharpen his beak on a slice of apple, attacking it with sharp little jabs.

Yes, today I feel light under the blubber. It's like when you finally extract the wormy, white, thready trail of a blackhead. I am inexplicably satiated with the agreeable feeling of being exactly where I should be. Maybe Belgium is the home of sweet torpor, of beatitude, where one can in fact die a good death.

At this very moment there are certain people in Paris who are in the midst of papers about the theme of paternity in the works of Balzac[50], of reverie in Jean-Jacques Rousseau[51]. How good it is not to be one of them. The Student is probably perplexed by my absence, since he knows that exams are but child's play to me. These exams, at any rate. I remain an abject and eternal failure when it comes to the test for admission into presentable society. I take pride in that failure, and in proclaiming it long and loud. A contrary coquette, enamored only of fashions lost to her fat-sheathed body, congratulating herself for sullying the starched purity of decent clothing. An ugly little thing, already old, or maybe a fat old whale made young again. I have nearly achieved my goal, and that is satisfying. I need only to perfect my extravagances to complete the work. The results so far are quite promising. Ah, here comes the Belle Otéro[52] sundae: two vanilla breasts with nipples of candied cherries, nestled in a bed of Grand Marnier-infused whipped cream and spread with a coverlet of toasted almonds and slices of kiwi fruit.

—

I am balancing on one foot. The platform of the scale shook at first, but is now steady. The needle rotated brusquely toward one hundred. For a fraction of a second, I catch a mental glimpse of my mother, ugly. A crack of lightning, under your rouge, two badly adjusted halves of the mask of your face, fractured lengthwise by a shock of electricity. You resemble me. Mirrored, we weigh the same in obstinacy and silence.

To outdo you, I take huge mouthfuls.

—

A break in my insomnia. The hotel room is so lethally dull that now I fall asleep as soon as I get into bed.

—

I awoke again this morning with the agreeable sensation of having done something worthwhile with my life: the well-being of accomplishment. But I must not get complacent, nor lose sight of the goal.

I should think about going back to Paris. It is only inside the shell that one finds the limp, milky mussel who wants to grow larger than the whale.

—

For the return trip, a stash of white chocolate. A long ribbon of twisted licorice, like the kind children gnaw on at the end of the school day. A few packets of shortbread.

I am unlearning to talk here. In Paris, there are long conversations with The Student from time to time. My voice is getting weak. Shopkeepers ask me to repeat my requests, and tenuous string of chaotic, discordant noise emerges from my mouth, as if from the bottom of a bag of cotton balls.

Soon I will decide when speech will no longer be of any use to me.

—

On the train. Severe fatigue. Somnolence, almost for the entire journey, except when I needed a chocolate from my bag. Fatigue. And soon I'll have seven flights of stairs to climb. I have a feeling that I'm really making strides toward the end. But does the best or the worst still await me?

—

Paris is close now. The Student is there somewhere, with his beautiful pianist's hands. With his large somber eyes. Why?

—

I can't stop thinking of sugar.

—

I haven't been back to class since my return from Brussels. I have absolutely no desire to make my way through the crowds of students, to try and block out their chattering noise, pedantic and humorless. Although it was my own decision to enroll there, I've never liked the school. My father was right: it was the choice of the mediocre. This way, by the way, one of the few times he's expressed anything remotely like an opinion about my concerns. He would have preferred, for the sake of prestige, that I enter a professional school. I certainly had the aptitude for it. But the ghetto of advanced courses would have wiped out any chance for anonymity or flexibility in my schedule. I would have to have been answerable to them for my work. I answer to no one, except this journal, and it doesn't demand any accountability at all. The perfect friend. The ever-available and always-patient ear. It registers without distorting. It knows how to keep a secret. It doesn't judge, or meddle, or try to help me, or cure me, or transform me, or make me change my ways. It gives me the chance to not forget the language of my race. It offers the freedom and luxury of uninterrupted words. It spares me the exhaustion of human contact: inquisitive, gossiping, prying, questioning, demanding justifications, vindications, details, whys, hows. It displays its blank white pages without fail and with the greatest generosity, the utmost neutrality. It accepts me as I am but do not yet wish to be. Who else in the world would tolerate my physical and mental deformities this way—my sarcasm, my demands, my desperate hunger for death and my insatiable taste for sugar? This Other does not exist, some perfect entity who watches over me with an unspoiled, uncorrupted eye. The Student is nothing but an *other*.

——

The Student. I'll bet my absence is worrying him. I know he thinks about me, for reasons I cannot comprehend. Perhaps monstrosity fascinates him. Does he possess that Baudelairean taste for the hideous and the bizarre? I have unknowingly been wielding a power that escapes me, the consequences of which I cannot measure. I reassure and I disturb—the beautiful in their beauty and the ugly in their ugliness.

——

I think of him, often. The way I'd think of a marvelously constructed pastry so elaborate and artistic that you hardly dare plunge in your spoon for a taste, for fear that its flavor can't possibly measure up to its exquisite appearance. Or one of those huge Easter eggs whose decorated shell you have to crack open in order to see what's inside, but you wish you could eat the contents

without having to destroy the egg. Or those trick fruits
and cakes that present a deceitfully attractive colored
exterior, but betray their promise of sweetness with the
taste of salt or pepper, acidity or bitterness. You can't
trust anyone.

—

My room. A jumble of books that I never open anymore,
piles of unwearable clothing, sugary victuals that are
haphazardly stacked here and there as I buy them, empty
cookie packets, papers I should have thrown out a long
time ago. A pyramid of cans containing fruit preserved
in heavy syrup was blocking the mirror. I've just finished
moving them so I can see myself in the glass. I've given a
lot for this skin. The sallow complexion, the puffy cheeks
blotched with a wide array of pimples. My head is like an
over-yeasted brioche on the verge of splitting open. The
only cavities in this plump relief are the huge purple-gray
circles around my eyes. A sausage in a too-tight dress.
I can almost count the rolls of fat beneath the material,
which is about ready to rip apart at the seams. My self-
allotted morphology satisfies me. I do not frighten myself.
Only the rest of the world is intimidated.

—

My hallucinating eyes scrutinize the night tirelessly, like
a she-wolf. The farther back in time my mind goes, the
more the thick silence of the night closes in around me…
it makes me hungry. I never stopped walking on four
legs, ear to the ground, nose following the invisible trail
of my peers. The glare of the festival lights can't reach
the deserted hallway of the third floor, and the violins

in the orchestra are muffled into vague mewling. From
the ends of the flower-strewn alleys and across lighted
terraces comes the din of mundane conversations. From
time to time I catch the stealthy echo of frayed laughter
not meant for my ears. And yet, I have not once heard
the voice or the laugh of a child. We, the short, eternally
excluded from nocturnal celebrations, our nannies having
drowned us in the black liquor of sleep. But rocking
chairs, like those boxes of candy left on my nightstand,
have never lived up to their rumored capabilities in my
case. Indomitable and unsuspected insomniac that I
am, I have explored solitary nooks and hidden crannies
wherever I go, without ever encountering another soul.

Except one. Only once.

It was The Spaniard.

But I am too thirsty now. My page has drunk its ration of
ink, but I haven't yet had my share of anisette syrup.

—

The neighbors are fighting again. It's a habit now. I hate
their insults and their screams, devastating and petty
opposites of the higher emotions. These are the crumbs
of an unraveling private life that I am forced to sweep up.
They are planting thorns in my garden of silence. They
invade my space without ever apologizing, absorbed in
game that has no umpire, in which all blows are fair.

I hate their cries, all cries, anything that howls and fights
and makes war upon itself. Anything that pierces my
heart, slices open my memory and makes it bleed its bitter
juice.

—

Under the canopy of flowers, a great cold violence.
A crescendo of searing words, none of which I can
understand. My mother, as beautiful as any morgue
aesthetician could make her. The boil is eating away
at least half my chin. I hold my breath to keep my
presence secret. I can see The Spaniard face-on. This
time he inspires no terror in me, because he is emanating
something pained and pathetic, which is somehow
reassuring. He is begging my mother, his voice rising.
He wants to see the little girl. He wants to see me. He
repeats my name. They quarrel. They lower their voices
until they are almost spitting their words, suffocating on
them. They threaten each other frantically. They argue
on, locked in a struggle I can't hope to comprehend. They
are lost in their hatred. Somehow I am at the center of
that hate. Terribly innocent, yet dreadfully culpable, there
behind the privet hedge. How long did it go on? Until the
cry. Until the slap across the face.

My mother's cry, expulsed along with her gesture, from
the depths of her hatred. Then a petrified silence. And
finally, The Spaniard's sobs.

Pus erupted from the boil.

—

White spots are cropping up all over my face, embryonic
boils, thanks to my horrible diet. They're like smallpox,
which can be the price of sweet pleasures. Perhaps I'll
die like Louis XV after all: by the means through which I
have sinned.

No complaints. No groans. Sarcasm before groans. Irony before complaints. I will die of indigestion, snug and warm under my coverlet of fat. Happy.

—

The rest of the night was quiet. Troubling. I can recall the tiny sprays of sand that the wind threw sporadically at the half-open blinds. The continuous crackle of the light bulb under the lampshade. The insane doggedness of mosquitoes hurling themselves at the netting over the bed. ("Why," my mother once asked, "must we always live in places infested with mosquitoes?")

The book fell out of my hands when The Spaniard came tiptoeing into my room. Nothing seemed more natural to me than his presence here at my side, and I thought it was in no way odd that he should remove his shoes, so he should make no noise in the hallway. Kneeling by my bed, he rested his head on my arm. "Don't tell anyone I was here. It's a little secret, just between us…"

The newly forming bald spot in the middle of his skull suggested a huge gleaming eye bristling with thick lashes. My fingers ventured there. His hands were a bit damp, or maybe mine were. Our dampness mingled, as did our breath. Never since then have I known such gentleness, such a peaceful sense of intimacy.

He saw the barley-sugar sweets on the nightstand, and the box of chocolates in its silvery wrapping paper.

"Is it her?" he asked, under his breath.

"I don't like candy," I confided, whispering in his ear.

"Then I shall give you something better."

He pressed his lips into my wide-open palm, then closed my fingers over it again.

"Keep this kiss always. In remembrance of me."

He left just as he had come. For always. Today, in my hand, there is a jumble of lines—some thready, some deep—the maze of my life, to which I have finally found the exit.

—

The Student's hair is nearly as dark as The Spaniard's. A lovely, inky black. Black as a scorpion. And you know, my own hair is as dark as my father's is blond.

—

An apocalyptic vision of my desiccated corpse decaying on a beach in the South Seas. The untamed whale. No one will know I am dead. No one was informed of my departure. Some sailors hoist me onto the cargo deck with grappling hooks. The captain and crew do not doubt for an instant the danger I represent. When the boat docks after their long voyage, they come looking for me down in the hold to unload me. I have eaten the entire cargo of bananas and pineapples, and they are ruined. Thanks to my elasticity, I can still squeeze through the doors. I try to escape but my bulk soon weighs heavily on my legs. They are able to recapture my fairly quickly. They beach me on the shore and rend open my belly with a single sharp thrust of a harpoon. My sugary entrails twist out onto the sand in an olive-green mass. Not even a turtle would want it for her starving children's breakfast. My carcass cooks slowly and gently in the tropical sun, taking on the architectural whiteness of a meringue. I look closer. My skeleton is fragile, robbed of its spongy envelope of flesh. And now I sleep for all eternity. I dream of my bladder bursting into the open air. Tatters of my skin flutter in the wind like failed crêpes, then fly off to stick to the faces of Mama and her friends. They all scream louder than if snakes or rats were slithering between their legs. They asphyxiate as their nostrils are deprived of air, inhaling instead shreds of my skin. They breathe in millions of my scraps. I am inexhaustible: this poisoned flesh, born of woman's flesh.

—

I am also a glutton for delirium. The only unpredictable part of my remaining time is the visions—they will be a surprise as massive as a vacherin[53] prepared for a first Communion.

—

The wedding cake has been ordered. Twenty guests, three slices apiece. It should be quite tall.

A baker's apprentice should be delivering everything any second now.

Tonight I am getting married. I am celebrating my union with my beloved sugar. The pact has been signed and sealed for long time now, lacking only the solemnity of a true ceremony. I hear someone coming up the stairs. Then nothing. The apprentice seems to be listening for the sounds of a party for guidance. Again the footsteps. Hesitation. To the right? The left? A wedding celebration on this floor? Bizarre. The footsteps stop in front of each door. He must be reading the names as he approaches. Here it is! He knocks.

Fate, when she knocks, knocks brutally. It is her function to intervene when the protagonist least expects her. And therein lies her charm, diabolic though it may sometimes be. People accuse her of disrupting their plans. But really, without her, life would be awfully dull.

When, instead of the cake, I found The Student at my door, I was struck with the memory of one of history's great romantic moments—the impossible marriage of Jane Eyre[34]! Another solitary afternoon of boredom, in London probably, and Charlotte Brontë made my heart race with such emotion! I will give Mama credit—she always got me to read the native authors of whatever country we were stationed in. I wouldn't try re-reading the novel now, for fear of blunting the edge of the feverish thrill induced by those pages. The wedding scene—what a lovely bit of tragedy that was! As the reader and the assemblage expect the ritual, that fateful "yes", a man's voice comes from the back of the church and declares that the marriage of Jane Eyre and Mr. Rochester cannot take place. A superb incarnation of Fate, this man brings forward proof of his claim: Mr. Rochester is already married, and his wife is a madwoman! And so The Student asked around, tracked down my lair, and thus discovered the site of my secret wedding.

He, the handsome, the unexpected, the unacceptable, is here. I have the stabbing feeling of being caught red-handed in some awful lie. A stampede crashes through my head. It's as if the safety of a gun has been released and shots are ringing uncontrollably through my brain.

Claude Tardat

Excuses, explanations, justifications all superimpose
themselves upon one another in the space of a heartbeat.
Palpitations, quivering knees. He is there, at my door. A
grain of sand blown by the winds of destiny into the well-
oiled cogs of the machine that is my solitary tranquility.
An event. Let him in—keep him from coming in—the
wedding cake will be delivered right before his eyes—
the ceremony is in jeopardy—Jane Eyre—the course
of my whole life turned upside down. Come up with a
lie. Get him to leave quickly. Thieving my solitude. Say
something. Say anything. Say I have a fever, a contagious
illness, pinkeye, anything, the doctor or nurse is coming
to give me a shot. He cannot be allowed to witness my
universe of honey and compote. My notebook lies open
on the table, the page still glistening with fresh ink. I don't
want anyone here. Nobody. But it's him. Decide now—
yes or no. I must take up the reins of my own life, of my
own death. It is I who will decide, not him—not him, not
the unexpected. Go away. Settle off any debts, forever, for
always. It's because I was in Brussels. And the literature
exams? The hell with them—I don't think it's possible
for me to care any less about them than I do now, if you
want to know the truth. The delivery boy could be at the
bottom of the stairs this very minute, looking for my name
on the mailboxes. Is this really where the cake is supposed
to go? Deny it—deny it outright. I've paid in advance,
after all. No, there must be some mistake—I never
ordered such a thing—and anyway, nobody gets married
in a dump like this—see, no party here. Or else make
The Student come in, tell him everything—he's welcome
to share the cake with the imaginary guests—doesn't it

look delicious?—take a piece! Change the point of the ceremony maybe? Or provoke him—throw my anger in his face, make him actually look at the monster, see the creature standing here in the middle of a rug littered with cookie crumbs, surrounded by shelves groaning under the weight of jam jars. My lips are soiled with chocolate—he could even taste the monster here in this garbage heap of empty candy wrappers. He has given himself so much grief trying to pry the Beast out her shell, playing with sugared fire—he has the best of intentions, and he will pay me back for all of it—my baptismal, wedding and funeral rites all rolled into one. Such disarray. I have no room for the unexpected. Sorry, too late. I am mute. It lasts several interminable seconds.

In the face of my unbearable, absolute distress, his disarming simplicity appears, along with the unhoped-for salvation he unwittingly offers. "Oh—were you writing?"

He had seen the open notebook and uncapped pen laid between its pages from his position in the doorway. "So that's why you've been playing dead! You've been writing!"

I shrugged my shoulders wordlessly, letting him create a lie for me—a golden excuse, an alibi that only magnifies me in his eyes. "You're right. When you have a gift, you should use it. I'm sorry if I interrupted your train of thought. I'll come back and see you some other time."

I said I'd meet him at the Viennese bakery tomorrow.

—

Overwhelmed by his other delivery orders, the baker's boy showed up an hour later, ashamed to have made me wait.

—

Spangled with silver pearls, cemented together with nougatine[55], then lacquered over with caramel, the cleverly constructed edifice is enthroned on a platform in the middle of the rug. I haven't touched it yet. I have the whole night to celebrate the marriage service. By dawn, the strength to write may have abandoned me. That's why I've just written everything down about The Student's visit. And so I don't forget that I've promised to meet him. One thing bothers me about this cake, one inevitable accessory that I should have foreseen. The baker planted the traditional figurine of the wedding couple upon the summit of his creation. He is all in black, she is dressed in white. They are holding hands, both imprisoned behind the same plastic smile, crimson and vapid. A naïve image of humanity's greatest illusion. For what can these two do now, having risen so high, but come back down the long sticky slope of the mountain, getting their little paws trapped by the flypaper that is life? They are incurably blind, obstinate in their denial of the deterioration of their one moment of glory. In their profound deafness they do not hear the swan discreetly slip the first notes of its song into the grandiose accents of their wedding march.

—

But I see, I listen, I speak. I speak the painful truth of the twin pillars of despair: impermanence and lies.

Under the canopy of the honor guard, my father smiles at his wife, while my mother smiles at all the men. For a while now, I've only wanted to see the heavy gilt surrounding that photo. Having inspected the frame, my memory now fixates on my father's mane of golden hair. His iceberg eyes. His cold silence as he gazes upon me, contemptuous up at the heights of his Viking splendor: the brown dwarf with the dull complexion, already oily. The tiny, ignorant fiend who lifts toward him the indelible stain of her own licorice-drop eyes.

My inky eyes. And the little parcels of pink bonbons furtively secreted next to the bedside lamp. The venomous black of a scorpion.

Midway through my twentieth year, the import of the evidence has finally struck home. Stupid creature! I am the unwitting incarnation of a betrayal. Suddenly, I no longer have a name. Anonymous among the anonymous. I realize that I don't even know The Spaniard's name.

—

This monster that I have built out of lard will slip a ring of fidelity onto its finger and devour all sixty pieces of wedding cake, which are filled with curaçao cream.

—

The marriage has been consummated. It was hard to go all the way, I confess. Vertigo. My head is heavy. I am feeble and tense. Mustn't forget to go meet The Student. Sleep now, if I can.

Encumbered by so much flesh, I can't find a comfortable position.

Writing again. I occupy myself with finding exactly the right word, so I won't hear the accelerated heartbeats echoing in my chest, and so the ball of lead wedged in the pit of my stomach can find its way out.

Here's a preview of what I'll say to The Student.

My penultimate lie: I'm going to go to Madagascar for a while to see my parents;

final lie: when I get back, I'll offer to let him be the first to see whatever it is he thinks I've been writing. This will be a way of thanking him for his zeal and attention, and a reward for attributing so much talent to me;

then commit his face to memory, his body, his features, one by one, as provisions for the sugary journey;

pay the bill for the last cakes we shall ever eat together, and say goodbye normally—certainly not an adieu—since I doubt he'd be fooled otherwise (okay, one more lie, then);

and leave without looking back, even though I know I shall want to (and a new lie, but to myself).

———

Soon it will be time.

The only dress I can still get on is crushing me like a corset.

—

Everything went just as I planned, except for an urge to cry when he asked if we could meet again soon. But I swallowed the salty poison of my tears just in time.

I warned The Student that he wouldn't be getting any postcards. Obviously. Now it's time to get on with it, to hurry things long. How many journeys to make before that ultimate voyage? How many trips up and down these goddamned stairs to fill the room to the rafters with the necessary supplies? My legs are already starting to buckle under the immense weight of my buttocks. A little life escapes me with every flight I ascend.

With a massive effort, I push the table, which has served me so well as a desk, next to the bed and haul several boxes of now-useless books down to the trash. My room will soon be reduced to a narrow corridor running from the bed to the door.

I'm done with fresh-baked pastries, ice cream, sorbet, flavored yogurt, seasonal fruit. I must hold a wake for my perishables. And thus do I enter the demesne of preserves, dry cookies, mummified sugar, cellophane, and can-openers.

Of course, that still leaves plenty to die from.

—

I'm stockpiling. I haven't come near to finishing the provisioning process. The room is far from full. You can't imagine how many packages of cookies, how many jars of honey and jam, how many bags of candy and bars of chocolate it takes to fill up even a cramped little hovel like this. I've been hoarding for days. I've also been eating twice as much as usual so I don't lose any weight with the forced exercise.

—

The mirror is going to disappear. I look at myself one last time in the full horror of my nudity. I ponder all the effort it's taken to get to this point. To create this blasphemous, unspeakable thing that is me.

—

My private parts are now buried under an unbreachable depth of flesh. The Student's hand would be lost in between the giant gourds of my breasts, or forced to forage through granules of snow to find the entrance to the igloo in the cleft of my frozen, fossilized legs. Nothing to be found there—not snow after all, but shattered and broken crystals of sugar.

—

I do wash occasionally. I can't actually reach all of my body parts now. My hair is plastered down in a greasy, glossy band. My dark hair, black like licorice juice.

—

The fairies who came to my cradle endowed me with the gift of disproportion, that strange and terrible instinct that renders children insatiable. And I will die of it. There will be nothing left of the masterpiece that is my life but an execrable pulp that will soon blacken and rot beneath six feet of earth. A feat of engineering am I, constructed of sugar, nibbled upon by worms. I will rest unknown, but

in a form that never went unnoticed. Artists die in the
shadows. It is their lot. Only eternity will allow me to live
out my extravagant excesses.

—

I think I can say that I probably would have been
comfortable living a life of obesity.

—

A difficult night. A persistent little mosquito plunges
into the abundant pleasures of my flesh. Ironically, and
perhaps incredibly, I do not use the force of my bulk
against the insect.   I am suffocating, like the fat
nannies in Martinique, the ones that Mama would point
out to me in the street sometimes. I was maybe eight
years old—the chronology escapes me. Mama said, "God
forbid my daughter should ever be like them!"

My mother. I can hardly imagine myself in her body—so
fragile, so nervous—tense and languid all at once.

Was it I who emptied her of her blood, her water, her
milk? She also said to one of her friends, unaware that
I could hear them, "It was pure luck that motherhood
didn't leave a single trace on me—I'm back to the same
body I had as a girl! Not even a stretch mark."

The Larousse encyclopedia later instructed me about the
nature of stretch marks.

—

Extreme fatigue. I know now that I won't be going out
any more. It's difficult even to write. Empty jelly jars are

piling up all over the place.　　　　There are constant sparks of acidity in my stomach. Sweet bubbles of gas rise in my throat. I bite my fingers.

—

A recipe suggestion for writers who want to add some weight to their words, some heft to their writing: dip your pen in a mixture of sugar and ink. If it doesn't work, you can always console yourself by just drinking the rest of the potion.

—

The level of provisions in front of the mirror has gone down, because that's the side I attacked first. I'm getting tired of my own face now that I've found it again. A pumpkin head, dirtier and dirtier. The rest of me should reappear in a few days.

—

Unstoppable hiccups mark off the time I have left. Brief lulls in the storm prove that I'm still breathing. It's either too hot or too cold in the room, and a line of verse by Mallarmé[30] has been singing through my head for days, like an incessant buzzing saw. "The flesh is sad, alas, and I have read all the books."　　　　What is the state of the soul? Nothing other than the state of the stomach.

—

Pain along my ribs, worsening with my continued lack of sleep.

—

How long is it since I showed any sign of life to the outside world? I'm sure there's a note from Mama in my mailbox, but I just don't have the strength to go downstairs. My handwriting is getting bad—prickly, angular. Like the footprints of a scorpion.

—

Breathing is getting increasingly difficult. Am I nearing the end?

—

I am fascinated with myself. I observe the proliferation of fat and pain with lucid detachment, the cold interest of the entomologist examining a gnat caught in a spider's web. I have never been whole. There is the one machine that thinks, and the other that digests. The one watches, the other engulfs. When exactly did I consent to this?

—

The crushed strawberry of my first menstruation, discovered in the heat of a tropical morning. The sun flooded the room, making the stain of hemoglobin all the more obvious on the white sheet. The air was so heavy, the same consistency as the night of The Spaniard's visit to my room. I am thinking of him, now that the peonies no longer fall from between my thighs. Ruby blood. Blood like pomegranate syrup. The gift of a generous and painterly god. The juice of all fruits, hot secret sap that only flows from wounded flesh, denouncing its own scandal, its own shame.

Claude Tardat

Blood is too beautiful to be spilled, which is why I've chosen not to simply open up a vein. Anyway, that would have made a mess of the sheets.

—

I don't hear the neighbors anymore. Maybe they're on vacation. I don't meet anyone on the landing. To each his own petty life, petty pleasures, his own shameful illnesses, down to the amount of sugar he puts in his coffee. The toilet at the end of the hallway seems miles away. Mama's body doesn't make noises. It sings.

Clouds of gas forming in my gut, compact and chaotic, hurling themselves at the unchanging contours of my ribcage. Despite my bulk, I still have the skeleton of a child.

Nausea.

Someone knocks on the door. They try opening it—the knob turns in one brusque motion. Someone has decided to come find me. Someone in a hurry. The concierge? The landlord? I paid my rent in advance so I wouldn't be disturbed. Is it The Student?   Crystal by crystal, my life is coming undone.

—

What unknown liquor will spring from the fermentation roiling permanently in my bowels? I am a distillery now. Mama would nurse a glass of punch or whiskey for hours. Zohra told me so. I don't remember when or why. Over the course of an evening, she would refill her glass with ice, on top of the alcohol she hadn't drunk.

120

A Sweet Death

The contents were irrelevant. Only the glass—and the maintenance of that glass—had any importance. Her red fingernails, perfectly manicured, were plastered to it. A crucial accessory for striking her poses and inventing her seductive gestures. Alcohol scared her. Above all, she feared the tiny veins and blotches that drink might bring, an irremediable blossoming along the sides of the nose.

I don't drink. I only really know alcohol from its fragrance in creams and cakes. And yet I have the waxy complexion and bloated body of a dipsomaniac actress. But there is no-one to pay attention to my bankruptcy, moral or otherwise. I am a celebrity only in my own eyes.

—

Is it the pen that's so heavy, or is it my hand?

I'm not even hungry for sugar. Too many cookies......

—

Again with the hiccups that rock the aqueous edifice of my gut. Overfull with liquid, shaking with the fearless gallop of a wild horse. Fatigue. Dizziness.

—

Every day I'm shocked when I greet myself in the mirror. That deformed ogress is me. Sometimes I ask myself if the most monstrous part of this whole thing isn't the gaze I set upon that creature in the glass.

—

How many days without the strength to write?

—

It was The Student who knocked. Like last time, he tried to open the door. Now he's calling out to me. How did he find out I'm not in Madagascar? Did he guess? Did he sniff out my lies? Can he smell the stench of my entrails through the door? He has no business in this grotesque cavern. He's the beautiful one, the negation of all that I am. He belongs in the realm of perfumed arbors, tennis courts, music, freedom from care. He knows how to smile. He loves life and makes the most of it. I would like to tell him as much—simply and without bitterness— somewhere besides within these walls, somewhere other than this nauseatingly foul-smelling room. On the corner of a bench in some charming tea-room. Too late.

He is too late now to plant the seed in my mind that maybe I'm making a terrible mistake.

I must remember to lock the door when I come back from the toilet.

—

So heavy, and yet so very empty.

—

Another little mouthful of carbohydrates. My faithful companions in these nights of insomnia. The precious fuel for my nocturnal meanderings. I try to write, to forget how sick I feel. I try eating.

—

Some greedy vermin is burrowing restlessly into my gut. It suckles pure sugar from my mammary glands. The

Student. Will he come back? I've chosen sugar and its slow sweetness, tiny gulps of pleasure. I've had a tea party with Death. At the end of this unraveling night, I just want to give up, have someone bring me a bowl of hemlock, a cyanide capsule, a poisoned arrow. Let the scorpion do its work, as had once been foretold.

Oh Zohra! Why did you have to meddle?

My life is trapped in a heavy snare from which there seems to be no escape, and no return. I am the antithesis of mystery. I am clothed only in my nudity now.

—

Several days of constipation. I feel like there are wads of shit piling up into my chest. All this because of some ink stain.

—

Day after day without writing. My head cracks with migraines. Chewing echoes in my skull like some hellish machine gun. I quell the pain with more sugar.

—

My stomach is stuffed full. It gurgles like mad. Unable to find any repose, I find myself constantly in front of the mirror. I can't even keep myself company anymore.

—

The monster has attained an exquisite degree of abomination. In vain. Because no one will measure the actual value of the enormous effort it took me to surpass mere monstrosity. Only these illegible words, running into and over one another, can truly bear witness to the worth of that work   My poor invertebrate hand.

I have squared the circle. I will go no further.

—

I can tell the end is very close now. I will load my last cartridge of ink. I bequeath this pen to…to whom?
         My throat is burning. I keep having the same dreadful thought— that I have swallowed a scorpion. And Zohra isn't here. My teeth are chattering. A frozen she-wolf tangled up in her own teats.

Daybreak. A cold light on the rooftops. I watched each hour of the night pass along through the open window. My tongue, heavy with chocolate, sticks to the roof of my mouth. A rancid taste overwhelms my palate.
What if death is tasting this vile taste for eternity, never leaving my mouth?

What if death is nothing but endless insomnia in the heart of a slumbering city?

—

Someone was knocking. The Student? Or maybe I dreamed it? Everything is muffled. Voices aren't coming through. They say an excess of sugar will make dogs go blind.

—

Death should be sweet. Like sugar.

—

The ribbon of the amulet, which has been strangling
me the last few days, finally breaks. When she put this
strange jewel around my neck, with its reek of cloves and
eucalyptus, Zohra said, "It will keep away the evil spritis."

—

Where is The Spaniard?

—

My eyes grow dim.

Notes

1. Frangipane: A pastry used in various desserts, made of milk, sugar, flour, eggs and butter. Also a type of cream filling into which ground almonds are mixed, and sometimes essence of bitter almond, to intensify the flavor.

2. Kim Cone: Brand name of a frozen treat consisting of an ice cream cone (usually with a scoop of vanilla) entirely dipped in chocolate.

3. Saint-Honoré: Dessert consisting of a layer of plain pastry, upon which is arranged a crown of profiteroles (see note 9), each of which is topped by a smaller, caramel-glazed profiterole. The hollow of the circle is filled with flavored Chantilly cream. Named for the patron saint of bakers.

4. Amandine: A fancy large tart (though sometimes made as several small tartlets) of sweet shortbread pastry with a filling of eggs, sugar, ground almonds, flour and butter, flavored with rum. After baking, an apricot jam glaze and candied cherries are put on top.

5. <u>Omelette norvégienne</u>: Dessert similar to Baked Alaska—ice cream coated in meringue and then browned in the oven.

6. <u>Millefeuille</u>: Dessert consisting of thin layers of puff pastry dough separated by layers of filling—typically custard, flavored cream or jam—then spread with white icing or fondant after assembly. Literally "a thousand leaves", referring to the many, many thin layers of pastry. Typically served in smallish rectangular pieces, millefeuille is sometimes made as a large round.

7. <u>Maillol</u>: Aristide Maillol (1861-1944), French/Catalan. Artist, started early as a painter but devoted most of his later career to sculpture. His primary focus was the female nude, using massive forms to represent its solidity and stability.

8. <u>Baudelaire/*Les fleurs du mal*</u>: Charles Baudelaire (1821-1867), French. One of the major poets of the Decadent movement, Baudelaire had a lonely, isolated childhood, but was noted to be highly precocious in his literary studies. He had a very close, complex relationship with his elegant, emotionally distant mother. As he grew older, he developed a macabre turn of mind and became a great admirer of Edgar Allan Poe and the Romantic painters. He began overspending his income, smoking opium and drinking. In 1857 he published *Les fleurs du mal* (*The Flowers of Evil*), a collection of poems considered by many to be his masterpiece. The poems touch on themes of melancholy, corruption, metamorphosis and the oppressiveness of mere existence. There is a great deal of imagery related to fragrances and odors, as well as of unwholesomeness and putrescence. He

went to Belgium in 1864 hoping to improve his fortunes, both financial and literary, but without success. He reportedly ended up hating his time in Brussels, and while there began drinking even more heavily. He suffered a massive stroke in 1866 while still in Belgium. He was returned to Paris, where he died a year later. The Pléiade editions are full of annotations, critical commentary, manuscript variations and references. They are bound in high-quality leather with gilding, printed on good bible-paper, and are sold in individual slipcovers.

9. <u>Profiteroles</u>: Small sweet buns made of puff pastry, filled with custard, ice cream, jam, fruit purée or Chantilly cream, then topped (or at least served) with warm chocolate sauce. These can be eaten as is, but they are also used as the basis for other desserts such as Saint-Honoré or croquembouches. The name comes from the word "profit" and originally denoted a small gift or gratuity.

10. <u>Moka</u>: Layered sponge cake, filled with butter-cream flavored with coffee and chocolate.

11. <u>Religieuses</u>: One of three different desserts. (a) A large cream-puff–like cake filled with chocolate or coffee-flavored custard and topped with a smaller cake, also filled. The whole arrangement is then frosted and decorated with piped icing. (b) Cream-filled éclairs covered in fondant and arranged in a pyramid on a pastry base. (c) A tart filled with apple and apricot jams and raisins, topped with a latticework crust. The first two take their names from the color of their frosting, which recalls the color of the homespun cloth of the habit of some orders of nuns ("religieuses"); the third from the latticework crust, which resembles the grille of a convent door. The narrator is almost

certainly eating one of the first two, given the "chocolate" descriptor.

12. <u>Baba au Rhum</u>: Raisin cake drenched in rum, then decorated with candied cherries and angelica (a tall aromatic herb related to parsley; only the stalks are candied).

13. <u>Congolais</u>: Small sweet cookie made of meringue and coconut, slowly baked in a low oven.

14. <u>Chaussons napolitains</u>: Hollow cylindrical cakes filled with layers of almond paste and fruit jelly, decorated with marzipan and candied fruit.

15. <u>Tête de nègre</u>: One of three different desserts. (a) Spherical dessert consisting of two meringue cookies stuck together with chocolate buttercream, coated with more chocolate buttercream, and then rolled in either grated chocolate or a mixture of grated chocolate and coconut flakes. (b) A dome-shaped rice-based cake completely covered in chocolate sauce and surrounded by a ring of whipped cream. (c) A light, sweet pastry set atop a wafer cookie; the entire assemblage is then dipped into melted chocolate to hold it together.

16. <u>Kierkegaard</u>: Soren Kierkegaard (1813-1855), Danish. Theologian, philosopher and psychologist. Much of his philosophical writing deals with the importance of personal choice and commitment in determining the course of one's own life. His psychological works focus on exploring the emotions of individuals facing significant life choices. He is considered by some to be a proto-Existentialist, given his emphasis on

the individual, and how one's sense of relation to the world is grounded in self-reflection. He also discussed the notion of how the sins of parents end up affecting the lives of the children. Along with his numerous publications, Kierkegaard was an ardent private diarist, and he considered his journals to be his most trusted confidantes.

17.   <u>Rimbaud</u>: Arthur Rimbaud (1854-1891), French. Poet of the Decadent movement. Raised and educated at home (along with his siblings) by his mother, who isolated them from other children. He was sent to school at the age of nine, where he excelled in everything but math and science. His first published poem came out when he was 15, at which point he began acting out: drinking, stealing, writing obscene verse. He also produced some very well-reviewed poetry, which he said he accomplished via "a long, intimidating, immense, and rational derangement of all the senses." After a brief, debaucherous affair with another poet, Paul Verlaine (who tried to shoot him), Rimbaud wrote his masterwork, *Une Saison en Enfer* (*A Season in Hell*), a pioneering piece of Symbolist prose. He eventually gave up writing altogether after joining the army, and then becoming a coffee and arms merchant in Ethiopia. He died at the age of 37 of bone cancer.

18.   <u>Tarte Tatin</u>: Dessert consisting of apples sautéed in butter in a skillet, topped with a lid of pastry dough and then baked. To serve, the whole thing is flipped over so the fruit is on top. Sometimes made with pears, a tarte Tatin has an intense caramelized flavor due to the sautéing.

19.   <u>Mademoiselles Tatin</u>: Sisters Stéphanie and Caroline Tatin, who owned a hotel and restaurant in the Sologne, a rural region of north-central France, southwest of Paris. Legend has it that in 1898, Stéphanie created the first tarte Tatin (see note

18) when she became distracted while preparing a traditional apple tart and decided to fix the error by covering up the sautéed apples with a crust and putting the whole dish in the oven. It was a huge success and she continued to prepare the dessert. A Parisian restaurateur discovered the dish while staying at the hotel and took the recipe back to town, where it became a house specialty at the famed Maxim's.

20. Touron: A ring-shaped dessert made of egg whites, sugar, ground almonds and pistachios.

21. Loukoum: Also called rahat lokum (literally, "rest for the throat"), this is a variation on Turkish Delight, a soft jelly-like candy with a base of sugar, rose- and/or orange blossom-water, and nuts (usually pistachios or almonds). After being cut or molded into pieces, the candy is rolled in powdered sugar. Sometimes flavors and colors are added.

22. Cornes de gazelle: A cone-shaped pastry filled with ice cream, custard or Chantilly cream. Literally, "gazelle horn", due to its shape.

23. Diane Arbus: Photographer (1923-1971), American. Noted for her black-and-white portraits of socially marginalized people such as dwarfs, nudists, transvestites and circus sideshow performers. Her work has been criticized as being exploitative, but Arbus countered that the photos were taken with the full consent and cooperation of the subjects. However, she is said to have had later misgivings about a series of pictures she had taken of mentally challenged women. She committed suicide at the age of 48.

24. <u>Crème caramel</u>: Sweet custard tasting strongly of melted caramel. Similar to flan, but not necessarily browned before serving.

25. <u>Dostoïevski</u>: Fyodor Dostoevsky (1821-1881, Russian. Grew up on the grounds of a charity hospital where his father—a despotic former military surgeon—was a doctor. Jailed at 28 for being part of an underground intellectual group, he spent several years in a prison camp in Siberia. The inhumane conditions of the camp helped shape his beliefs in the virtues of suffering, humility and submission. He frequently wrote about dark, unhappy characters who were spiritually and psychologically tormented. He also discussed the idea that a positivist view of existence was utterly unrealistic. One of his famous works, *Notes from the Underground*, is written as the anonymous journal of an embittered proto-Existentialist.

26. <u>Tolstoï</u>: Leo Tolstoy (1828-1910), Russian. Considered one of the world's great novelists, Tolstoy is noted for his vivid, detailed descriptions of Russian life. He fought in the Crimean Wars, an experience which was instrumental in the development of his non-violent anarchism, in the model of Christ. Gandhi and Martin Luther King, Jr. both cited Tolstoy's ideas on this subject as influencing their own thoughts. Although he was born into the aristocratic class, Tolstoy renounced his wealth and privileged position toward the end of his life, with the intention of leading the life of a wandering ascetic, but he died before he could get started on his travels.

27. <u>Bulgakov</u>: Mikhail Bulgakov (1891-1940), Russian. Most famous for his novel *Master and Margarita*, in which Satan visits

Moscow in the 1930s to debate the existence of Christ and the Devil. It is typically seen as a critique of the corruption, greed, narrow-mindedness and paranoia of Soviet Russia. He also wrote several science fiction stories that are often read as indictments of a bungling Soviet government. Trained as a physician, he was aware that he would probably die young of the same hereditary kidney disease that killed his father, which he did.

28. <u>Tchekhov</u>: Anton Chekhov (1860-1904), Russian. Short-story writer and dramatist who was one of the first authors to employ the "stream-of-consciousness" technique. He also declined to embrace the idea that narratives should contain a definitive moral lesson; he felt the artist's task was to ask questions, not answer them. His first play, *The Seagull*, had a disastrously terrible premiere and was booed by the audience. However, several critics found it praiseworthy and felt that Chekhov might end up doing decent work.

29. <u>Macroûtes</u>: North African dessert similar to fritters, flavored with cinnamon and orange, filled with date or almond paste, and then drizzled with warm honey to serve.

30. <u>Corbeilles d'amour</u>: Bowl-shaped pastry filled with honey-infused custard, studded with almonds and pistachios. Literally, "basket of love".

31. <u>Znabias</u>: Tunisian/Moroccan variant of Egyptian *zalabias*, small golden fritters drenched in a syrup of orange-blossom water and rose petals.

32. *Le Beau et la Bête*: A play on *La Belle et la Bête* ("Beauty and the Beast") as "beau" is the masculine form of "belle" (handsome/ pretty). This is in reference to The Student's conventional attractiveness and the narrator's own perceived monstrosity.

33. Manuka: A very high quality honey from the flower of the manuka plant (*Leptospermum scoparium*), also called the tea tree. It is believed to have antibacterial and antifungal properties, can be eaten by some diabetic patients, and does not cloud. The tree grows almost exclusively in New Zealand and Australia. The honey is thought by many specialists to be one of the finest in the world, with a deep color and unusual flavor.

34. Renoir: Pierre-Auguste Renoir (1841-1919), French. One of the main painters of the Impressionist school. Many of his works celebrated the beauty of female sensuality, and he was especially fond in his later years of painting scenes of fleshy, young, nude women bathing. The work referenced in the novel, *La Danse à Bougival*, shows a couple at a country dance, which modern critics suggest is a scene of robust physical enjoyment.

35. Modigliani: Amadeo Modigliani (1884-1920), Italian. Painter and sculptor primarily noted for his elongated, mask-like portraits. Having been a very sickly, debilitated child, Modigliani was fairly sure he was going to die at a young age. His life of alcoholism, drug use and debauchery almost certainly expedited his demise.

36. Monsieur Proust: Marcel Proust (1871-1922), French. Novelist and critic most famous for his seven-part novel *A la Recherche du Temps Perdu* (translated originally as *Remembrance of*

Notes

Things Past, but more recently as *In Search of Lost Time*). Proust had a very close relationship with his mother, who encouraged his literary studies, while his father felt he should pursue a professional career. He began publishing at a young age and had a reputation as a snob and a dilettante. By 1910 he was at work on *Recherche*. Early on in the first book, the narrator has a bite of madeleine (see note 37) dipped in tea, which he recalls eating as a child. The sense memory of combined smell and taste inspires his plunge into the reminiscences that comprise the vast work. Proust died a veritable recluse in his parents' home, where he continued to live after they passed away.

37. <u>Madeleines</u>: Small soft cookies shaped like scallop shells and made of sugar, flour, butter and eggs. Sometimes delicately flavored with lemon. They achieved literary immortality in Marcel Proust's immense novel *A la Recherche du Temps Perdu* (see note 36).

38. <u>Pomme d'api</u>: Small, sweet red apples of Greek origin, brought to Western Europe during the Roman era. Often used to make caramel or candied apples. By extension, the term is sometimes used for the prepared fruit itself.

39. <u>Barbe à papa</u>: Cotton-candy, brightly colored and sometimes with added flavor. It first appeared at the 1900 World Exposition in Paris. Literally, "daddy's beard".

40. <u>Tour Saint-Jacques</u>: St. Jacques Tower is a 16th-century church tower originally sponsored by the wealth of Parisian butchers. It is an example of Flamboyant Gothic architecture and is covered with almost grotesquely elaborate ornamentation.

It was the Parisian starting point for pilgrims going to Compostela and the medieval alchemist Nicolas Flamel (who was rumored to have discovered the key to immortality, the Philosopher's Stone) is buried under its floor. Between general deterioration and the fact that it has been free-standing since the its church was demolished in 1797, the tower is not quite level (though not to the same degree as the tower in Pisa). Because of this the early Surrealist André Breton (see note 41) observed in his poem "Vigilance" that it wobbles like a sunflower.

41.   <u>André Breton</u>: Writer (1896-1966), French. One of principal founders of Surrealism, Breton was originally trained as a physician and psychiatrist. One of his first literary experiments was with automatic writing (in which the writer goes into a trance so his subconscious is producing the text). One of his main themes throughout his literary career was personal transformation. He also explored how people perceive and understand external events and objects.

<u>42.   Cadbury Fingers</u>: Wafer cookies made by the Cadbury sweets company. They are coated in chocolate and come in several flavors, including honeycomb, toffee and mint chocolate. So named as they are the same size and shape as human fingers.

43.   <u>Chausson aux pommes</u>: Pastry similar to an apple turnover, with sliced apples, sugar and cinnamon folded into a blunt triangle of flaky puff pastry. The top is slashed for ventilation and the pastry is then fried and dusted with plain sugar. Literally "apple slipper (as in footwear)".

Notes

44. Jérôme Bosch: Hieronymus Bosch (1450-1516), Dutch. Little is known of this painter's early life and only about 25 surviving pieces can be definitively attributed to him. Much of his work is highly symbolic commentary on the corruption of the church at the time, expressed in surreal, dreamlike imagery. Contemporary viewers considered his paintings to be nightmarish and grotesque, even monstrous. More recent interpretation considers his work to be precise visual renderings of medieval metaphors and concepts rather than mere gruesome titillations.

45. The *Icarus* of Brueghel the Elder: *Landscape with the Fall of Icarus*, attributed to Flemish painter Pieter Brueghel the Elder (1525-1569), though analysis in the 1990s casts this into doubt. The painting references the legend of Icarus, who, using wings constructed of feathers and beeswax by his father Daedalus, flew too close to the sun; the wax melted and he fell to his death. The foreground of the piece is dominated by a farmer plowing his field, while the background is the sea and a few ships, while Icarus' legs can just be seen sticking out of the water. The painting has as its legend the Flemish proverb "And the farmer continued to plow…", alluding to humanity's indifference to and ignorance of the suffering of others: people go on with their own day-to-day lives regardless of what might be happening in the rest of the world.

46. XVIe Arrondissement: One of the 20 administrative districts of the city of Paris. It is home to many embassies and consulates, as well as a large number of the city's wealthy foreign residents. Several major sports venues are located in the 16th. About half its area is comprised of the Bois de Boulogne, the second-largest park in town. It is one of the richest sections of Paris and contains some the most expensive real estate in the entire country. The Arc de Triomphe and the renowned Trocadéro

district are also in the 16th arrondissement. For the narrator to be
roaming through the area, particularly inside a building, in dirty,
unfashionable clothing, and she herself unwashed and slovenly,
would be sure to attract attention, if not suspicion.

47.   <u>Bavaroises</u>. A cold dessert of egg custard thickened with
gelatin, mixed with whipped cream and/or purées of various
fruits. Other flavorings are sometimes added. The mixture is
then set to chill in a mold.

48.   <u>Charlottes</u>: (a) A hot dessert of puréed fruit poured into
a mold lined with buttered cake or bread, then baked. (b) A
cold dessert of custard or mousse poured into a mold lined with
ladyfingers soaked in coffee or liqueur, then chilled to set. Given
the warm weather and earlier reference to bavaroises, it is likely
the narrator is having the latter.

49.   <u>Fraisier</u>: Dessert consisting of two squares of sponge cake
soaked in Kirsch (cherry brandy), sandwiching a layer of Kirsch-
infused butter-cream and strawberries. The whole is then topped
with red frosting and garnished with sliced strawberries. Literally
"strawberry plant".

50.   <u>Balzac</u>: Honoré de Balzac (1799-1850), French. One of
the first realist authors. His masterwork is a collection of almost
100 novels, plays and stories called *La Comédie Humaine* (*The
Human Comedy*), depicting a broad spectrum of French society in
the post-Napoleonic era. He describes a vast array of morally
complex characters in keen, unfiltered detail. Balzac was sent
away to a wet-nurse almost immediately after he was born and
did not see his parents again until he was six. He was sent off

to school shortly thereafter, an unhappy experience as he had difficulty conforming to the norms of life at the school. He spent a great deal of time in what was essentially solitary confinement for disobedience; he was often not allowed books, which was even harder for the avid young reader. He attempted suicide at the age of 15 but upon entering university he found his outlook much improved, although he could never be termed an optimist. One of his stories, *Une Heure de Ma Vie* (*An Hour of My Life*), written in 1822, entails the narrator's precise catalogue of what is occurring around him, interspersed with deeper personal reflections inspired by the described minutiae.

51. Jean-Jacques Rousseau. Philosopher (1712-1778), Swiss. A voracious reader as a child (he spent hours a day reading with his father), Rousseau was one of the early figures of the European Enlightenment. Among his contributions to Western social and political philosophy were the defense of religious tolerance; the concept of the social contract—the view that man can be ennobled in a system of civic cooperation and equality, while immoderation and inequality will inevitably lead to corruption and degradation; educational reform such that learning should be suited to a child's individual development and aptitude rather than a system of rote memorization and corporal punishment for poor performance; and the importance of subjective thought and introspection. As he aged, Rousseau's mental health declined and he spent most of the last few years of life in a state of self-imposed isolation. On a side note, he was one of the first proponents of breast-feeding for children by their own mothers rather than by wet-nurses, for reasons of both health and emotional bonding between mother and child.

52. Belle-Otéro: A sundae made up of two large scoops of vanilla ice cream, each topped with a cherry, and otherwise

garnished with fruits, whipped cream and colored sauces. Named for a Spanish courtesan and dancer renowned for her voluptuous figure. One of her most famous costumes consisted of gemstones glued directly onto her torso, hence the dessert's resemblance to a pair of breasts.

53.   Vacherin: A cold dessert consisting of a ring of meringue and almond paste, filled with ice cream and/or whipped cream. It may have fresh or candied fruits, candied chestnuts or liqueur-soaked sponge cookies on top. The whole dessert is then decorated with Chantilly cream, candied flowers and fresh and/or candied fruits. Often served at christenings and first communion celebrations. The dessert takes its name from its resemblance to a variety of cow's-milk cheese, also called vacherin, which is shaped like a whitish mound with small multicolored mold tracings in the rind.

54.   *Jane Eyre*/Charlotte Brontë/Mr. Rochester: The English novel *Jane Eyre* by Charlotte Brontë (1816-1855) was published in 1847. Charlotte Brontë was born to a clergyman and his wife, the latter dying when the child was five. She was sent to boarding school, where the poor conditions and bad food left her sickly. She and her sisters Anne and Emily began writing stories of imaginary kingdoms and each eventually published under pseudonyms and later, their own names. Each died young, Charlotte at age 38 during her only pregnancy, and with a novel unfinished. *Jane Eyre* tells the story of an orphan, Jane, who is sent by her cruel aunt, Mrs. Reed, to a charity school where the children are ill and malnourished, and frequently abused. After her schooling, Jane eventually takes the post of governess at remote Thornfield Hall. Her charge is an orphan, Adèle, who is the ward of the Hall's master, Mr. Rochester. Jane and the moody, darkly handsome Mr. Rochester strike up a rapport, though she is sure he intends

to marry a wealthy neighbor. During the course of her time at Thornfield, strange laughter, footfalls and noises are heard some nights. One evening, a mysterious fire breaks out in Mr. Rochester's room and Jane saves him; the same night, a guest—Mr. Mason—is brutally attacked, bitten by his assailant. All of these occurrences are blamed on a servant, Grace Poole, who is said to be a drunkard. Jane is summoned to Mrs. Reed's home to attend the older woman on her deathbed. She discovers she has another uncle, who had sent for her years before, but Mrs. Reed kept this from her out of spite and cruelty. Upon her return to Thornfield, Mr. Rochester declares his love and proposes to Jane. Shortly before the wedding, Jane wakes one night, thinking she sees a savage-looking woman in her room, and gets out of bed to discover that her veil has been ripped in half. At the climax of the novel, the wedding ceremony begins, only for Mr. Mason to object, saying that Mr. Rochester is already married to his sister, Bertha Mason. Bertha is a violent madwoman who is kept locked up in an apartment in the attic; she escapes from time to time when Grace Poole is passed out from drink. Mr. Rochester asks Jane to run away to the south of France as his mistress, but she refuses and sneaks away in the dead of night. After days spent on the moors, she is found half-dead by the three Rivers siblings (St. John and his sisters Diana and Mary), who take her in and help her recuperate. She starts teaching at the village girls' school that St. John, a clergyman, runs as part of his church duties. After some while, he proposes to her so that she might go to India with him as a helpmeet in his missionary work, although he does not feel anything but brotherly love for her. At this point, it is revealed that the uncle who wanted Jane to live with him has died and left her a vast fortune, and that he is also the uncle of the Rivers siblings, so Jane also finds that she has relatives who are good and kind. She insists on sharing out the fortune left by their uncle. Jane agrees to go with St. John, but as his cousin, not his wife. Before they depart, Jane has the sensation that she hears Mr. Rochester calling to her, so she returns to Thornfield for closure. She finds the mansion to be a hulking, burnt-out ruin, as Bertha set fire to the house and then jumped off the roof to her death. Mr. Rochester was gravely injured trying to save her, and is now sightless and without one of his hands, recovering in a nearby hunting lodge. He fears that Jane will find him repulsive, but she assures him that she still loves him and that they can marry as equals now, which they do. Mr. Rochester regains his sight in time to see their first-born son. The novel is written in detailed, first-person perspective.

56. <u>Nougatine</u>: A sweetmeat made of light caramel syrup and crushed almonds and/or hazelnuts. It can be molded into shapes to decorate other desserts, or used as a filling to hold together layers of cake. In the latter case, egg whites are stirred in for consistency, and pistachios or preserved fruits may be added too. It can be mixed into pastry, or used in chocolate-making when layered with other crushed nuts and dried fruits (often apricots). In the setting of the novel, nougatine is used in its capacity as a cake filling.

57. <u>Mallarmé</u>: Stéphane Mallarmé (1842-1898), French. One of the major Symbolist poets, Mallarmé's work inspired the Dadaists, Surrealists and Futurists. He was famed for his literary and intellectual gatherings and for several years was considered one of the central figures of French aesthetic and cultural circles. His work is very difficult to translate at is relies heavily on multi-layered meanings and sounds, and includes a substantial quantity of puns, homophones and wordplay that often simply cannot work in other languages. Several of his later works contain carefully positioned blank spaces among the

text. While the narrator's use of spacing in this general section of the novel appears to be related to her increasing mental and physical debilitation, it is likely not a coincidence that a quote from Mallarmé is used here.

Translator's Afterword

The book you are holding represents the culmination of a pair of circuitous journeys through the wilds of both translation and publication. The adventure began when I was presented with a soft-papered, dog-eared copy of an obscure, out-of-print French novel and a request to translate it into English, as the only prior English-language version had also been out of print for nearly two decades and copies are near impossible to find. I am a lucky translator in that I have the luxury of picking and choosing the jobs on which I work, because I'm not dependent upon language projects for my financial livelihood.

This one looked interesting, so I said "oui", with the caveat that it would probably take a while. Thus began the long slog of translation, editing, refining and poring over the *Larousse Gastronomique*. After months spent in the company of the by-turns maddening, sympathetic and irritating-as-hell narrator, the final product sat in my cramped little hands. Near the end of this process, a conversation with my friend Vladimir, who manages a local press, led us to the decision to give publishing it a try. This in turn led to a whole new quest: tracking down the author, her representatives, or even someone in charge of her estate to discuss issues of rights. Letters and emails to the publishers of the original French edition of this novel, as well as to the houses that had produced her other two works, plus the publisher of the Spanish translation of this book, attempting to locate any kind of contact information, all led nowhere. Searches for biographical information were equally un-illuminating. Except for the fact that she was born in Morocco, had some theatrical experience and wrote three books between the mid-1980s to the early 1990s (which came from the blurb on the back of the book and the Bibliothèque Nationale entry on her second novel), I couldn't find anything about her. Not even the French version of Wikipedia had an entry on this mysterious woman. Another friend suggested that Claude Tardat might be a pen name, an idea that introduced a whole new layer of potential impenetrability into the mix. In the end, and after many discussions, we decided to make arrangements to account for any royalties that might accrue to the author, should she ever surface, and then forge on ahead with publishing the book you now have in your hands. This has been a long journey indeed, in which I got to play the role not only of translator, but proofreader, recipe reviewer, copy editor and detective, and which (thus far) has been worth every step. I'd like to thank Mom and Dad, Vladimir, Robert, Melody, Naomi, Gabriel, Third Place and Chromatophore Presses, the College Inn Pub and Ginger the Book Machine for helping me make this all happen, with a huge *merci mainte fois* to Claude Tardat herself, wherever she may be...

About the Author

Claude Tardat was born in Morocco and completed her studies in literature. She then spent several years working on theatrical productions, and subsequently taught French near the city of Lille in northern France. She is the author of *A Sweet Death* (1986), *Drunkenness* (1989), and *Agnès K* (1993).

About theTranslator

Erin K. Wilson graduated from Whitman College with a degree in French Language and Literature, and received her Maîtrise in Modern Literature from the University of Montpellier (France). She spent seven years as a project manager and staff translator for a language agency in Seattle, and still works as a freelancer. In addition to translation, she works at the University of Washington and a local pub. She also enjoys cooking, getting tattooed and traveling when she can. She lives in Seattle with her collection of books.

CPSIA information can be obtained
at www.ICGtesting.com
Printed in the USA
FFOW03n1329171217
44035063-43257FF